"I am convinced that you, Amy, are my only hope. Do not, I pray, disappoint me!"

"D-do you love me?" she dared to ask, afraid of his answer yet knowing that she could never accept his proposal without his affection.

Tipping her head back, he looked into her eyes, allowing her to read his own. "I need you—the day I do not see you I consider wasted. The idea of you leaving here is unbearable—is that love? Never having felt it before, I do not know from experience, but I suspect it is so."

Miss Standish sighed and nestled closer. "Oh, yes," she replied confidently, "that's exactly love."

As her head was still and her lips temptingly near, he bent his head and kissed her, a proceeding that Amy found profoundly satisfying.

Also by Jan Constant
Published by Fawcett Books:

THE BERINGER HEIRESS

THE ONLY HOPE

Jan Constant

FAWCETT CREST • NEW YORK

A Fawcett Crest Book
Published by Ballantine Books
Copyright © 1994 by Janis Dawson

All rights reserved under International and Pan-American Copyright Conventions. Published in the United States of America by Ballantine Books, a division of Random House, Inc., New York, and simultaneously in Canada by Random House of Canada Limited, Toronto.

Library of Congress Catalog Card Number: 94-94031

ISBN 0-449-22296-9

Manufactured in the United States of America

First Edition: June 1994

10 9 8 7 6 5 4 3 2 1

CHAPTER ONE

The lady who had been standing by the window watching, with some consternation, the tiny flakes of snow falling from a leaden sky, turned as the door opened and a young lady, accompanied by a fashionable gentleman, entered.

She had been expecting their arrival, for a post chaise pulled by two sweating horses had recently passed below the window and swept under the arch into the inn's yard. That all was not well with the couple was clear; the rather willful mouth under the fashionable poke bonnet was inclined to tremble with suppressed rage and the shoulders under the elegant rose pink spencer were decidedly tense, while the grip that the gentleman kept on his companion's elbow seemed almost jailerlike.

Involuntarily Miss Standish stepped forward out of the shadows and the girl, for she was little more, turned on her a wide-eyed, hunted look. Seeing a quietly dressed gentlewoman, she caught her breath and an expression of hope appeared in her blue eyes.

"Aunt Almeria! Fancy finding you here!" she gasped, and cast herself upon the older woman's bosom. "You are my only hope!" she breathed thrillingly.

Miss Amy Standish blinked, but refrained from glancing behind her to see whom the girl could be addressing. There was an unmistakable appeal in the large eyes fixed on her face and it was apparent that the young arms that clasped her were trembling.

"H-how glad I am to see you," she was told tremulously.

The gentleman, who had released the younger lady's arm with every sign of reluctance, gazed suspiciously from one to the other. "Who is this, Clarissa?" he demanded, baffled.

"Why, Lucius, surely you have heard me mention my dearest Aunt Almeria? Only think what a coincidence finding her here, *just* when I was wondering what to do."

"A coincidence, indeed," remarked Lucius, obviously with a hearty disbelief in such happenings.

"The greatest luck, to be sure," put in Miss Standish, surprising herself by feeling the need to take part in this odd conversation. She had rather liked the title bestowed on her, she found. "I've often found that aunts are prone to have their uses."

Clarissa sent her a grateful glance, but Lucius's gaze was a blend of puzzled suspicion and arrogance, which Amy Standish found she did not care for. There was a certain flamboyance about his dress of which she could not approve. The snowy folds of his cravat were a little too high for common sense, the capes of his driving coat rather too many, and his oiled light brown curls too carefully arranged for the best of good taste, she thought. And now that she looked at him more closely, she saw that he was older than she had first thought, at least one and thirty, and the girl, despite her fash-

2

ionable garb, could not be above sixteen or seventeen.

A suspicion that he was a fortune hunter eloping with an underage heiress entered Amy's head and she instinctively put her arm around the girl, leading her to the wide inglenook where a cheerful fire blazed.

"Warm yourself," she urged. "You must be chilled after driving in this weather." The girl crouched in front of the fire, holding her hands to the heat. "Forgive me," Miss Standish went on, "but I appear to have forgotten precisely the reason behind your journey."

Clarissa sent her traveling companion a look of loathing. "Mr. Gambrill was a-accompanying me from London, but I find now that I was mis-mistaken as to his motives." Her voice shook and she hurried on, as the gentleman in question sent her a far-from-kind look. "There is now no need for him to bother further. With you here, dearest Aunt, Mr. Gambrill, who is pressed for time, is released from all obligation in my affairs—"

"Don't be such an idiot, Clarissa, as to suppose that I would leave you alone in an inn," and here he included Miss Standish in his lowering gaze, "even with your aunt!"

To speak so, he was obviously known to her newly acquired niece, Amy noted, as he tossed his hat and gloves onto the table. "Clarissa dear," she began, in her most auntly manner, "pray remember your manners. Introduce me, if you please."

"I am Lucius Gambrill," the man put in before Clarissa could speak. "I am related to Clarissa's guardian. Sir Hugo Dysart has been kind enough to extend to me his friendship since I returned from

3

the Americas. And who, madam, are you, may I ask?"

Miss Standish started somewhat at the name and grew a little pale, but neither the girl nor gentleman noticed and she recovered after an almost imperceptible pause. "I am Am-Almeria Standish," she told him calmly. "We are related distantly on Clarissa's—" Here she paused a little, hoping that the girl would take the hint, and was considerably relieved when she heard herself immediately awarded to the maternal side of the family.

"Indeed. That may account for the fact that I have never heard of you," commented Mr. Gambrill truculently.

"Why should you have?" put in Clarissa quickly. "One cannot keep track of a far-flung family. . . . I had never heard of you, until you arrived on Hugo's doorstep!"

"We are a very large family," Miss Standish assured him. "I am one of thirteen—we can hardly remember our names ourselves," she said, inventing wildly. "And to be sure, it *is* a very tenuous relationship. More cousin than aunt, really."

"Mr. Gambrill, do you not think that you should be on your way?" inquired Clarissa sweetly.

"You have called me Lucius all summer," he reminded her testily. "And I have already remarked that I have no intention of leaving you in a common inn—"

"But, *Lucius*, have you forgot that Sir Hugo will be arriving any moment? Remember how concerned you were that he was hot on our heels."

A frown appeared on the pale face of the gentleman and he tapped his chin reflectively with the quizzing glass he had taken from his pocket. "Do

4

you know," he said thoughtfully, "I believe that it would be best if I stayed until Hugo arrives."

Clarissa stared at him in dismay. "Do not be so pea-brained!" she exclaimed. "What can you be thinking of? For the last two hours you have talked of nothing but avoiding a meeting—and in the most cowardly way! Why are you so brave suddenly?" she demanded suspiciously.

Mr. Gambrill divested himself of his overcoat, arranging it over a chair, and laughed a little. "Clarissa, dear child, always so melodramatic! Why should Hugo be anything other than grateful to me? I would not mention it among strangers"—he shot Amy a sly look—"but with only your aunt here, I can safely say that I have been the means of saving you from an unfortunate alliance."

"An unfortunate alliance!" Clarissa repeated shrilly. "Why, you traitorous toad! It was *you*—"

"Precisely. Who thwarted your taking flight to Gretna Green, with that greenhorn you imagine is the love of your life!" A thin smile curved his lips. "If I am not mistaken, you will have left a wild, impassioned note for Hugo to find, declaring your intentions."

Miss Dysart looked daggers. "You know very well, for I told you so, that I intended throwing myself upon Kit's mother's sympathy until Kit came home!" she cried. "It was *you*, you loathsome toad, who set off for Gretna!"

"What a silly chit you are, to think that anyone, except a half-wit, would believe such a story. Dearest Clarissa, you must be aware that I was only funning. Hugo will well understand that I was teaching you a lesson."

The truth of this struck Clarissa, who was momentarily silenced, staring at her tormentor with a darkling gaze. "Well, of all the jarvy tales!" she gasped indignantly at last. "I am persuaded that you meant to go to Gretna and only now have changed your mind because Aunt Almeria has put a spoke in your plans." She glared at the fair man, her bosom swelling with rage. "I am not surprised that you are still on the lookout for a wife, Lucius, for what female in her right mind would even consider a flibbertigibbet who tries to copy his cousin's style and only manages to make a monkey of himself!" Her eyes traveled over him scornfully. "And let me tell you that only a pea-brain would consider that waistcoat at all the thing!"

Lucius Gambrill stole an involuntary glance down at the black-and-yellow stripes of the offending garment that he had chosen with such care that morning, and flushed with anger, but before he could speak Clarissa attacked again.

"You are nothing more than a puffed-up gadfly," she declared. "With the taste of a callow youth!"

"That's rich—coming from a cit's daughter!"

Miss Dysart smiled loftily. "A *rich* cit's daughter," she corrected, her lip curling.

Amy Standish had watched this exchange with interest, feeling that the girl appeared quite capable of taking care of herself. The gentleman seemed about to explode with outrage, as he sought for words to reply to this indisputable fact. At that moment the landlord appeared in the doorway, coughing apologetically.

"Excuse me, sir, but will you be wanting something to eat?" he asked. "The Missis don't keep a particular table, you see, us not being in the way of receiving quality, regular like."

6

"A little cold meat or cheese and bread would suit admirably," put in Miss Standish. "My niece has had a long journey and would be grateful for a private room."

"There's a room ready upstairs. Plain and simple, not what you're used to, no doubt. Bessie here will take you up if you're so willing."

The ladies signaled their acceptance and followed a plump girl—her resemblance to him proclaimed that she was the landlord's daughter—up the short flight of narrow, twisting stairs to a low room under the thatched eaves. Most of the floor space was taken up by two beds, covered in worn but clean and bright patchwork quilts. Bessie knelt and put a light to the fire already laid on the grate before turning to leave the room. Miss Standish asked pleasantly if it was possible to have a pot of tea brought up.

"Now, Miss Dysart," she said, when they were alone, deliberately using her most governessy tone, "I feel a little explanation is called for."

Clarissa eyed her uneasily, clearly pondering the tale to tell.

"The truth, if you please," continued Amy implacably. "I assume that you have run away—and that Mr. Gambrill offered to accompany you."

"By bad fortune I met him at the booking office, where I was hoping to hire a chaise—" She broke off to consider deeply. "You can have no idea of how expensive it is! I own to being quite shaken. The proprietors must make a fortune!" She paused reflectively again. "I wonder if my trustees would consider my buying a coach line? After all to *drive* one is quite acceptable nowadays . . . and it is much

7

more sensible to accrue rather than to leave wealth in a bank."

Deep in thought, she nibbled the end of her finger and Miss Standish recalled her to the original subject. "You met Mr. Gambrill," she reminded her.

"Yes—he is some sort of cousin and so quite acceptable, you know. He would *not* go away and insisted upon hiring the coach and accompanying me, which I thought surprisingly kind of him, for to tell the truth, I had no idea that the whole affair would be so difficult ... or expensive. I was quite ashamed that I'd never liked him above half. I intended to go to Carley Weston, which is where Kit's mother lives, and throw myself on her bosom!"

"I see—and how would this lady have received your unexpected arrival?"

A sunny smile appeared on Clarissa's face. "She is the dearest person. We have known each other since my school days, so I have no doubt that she would have received me like a daughter."

Her listener had doubts. "I take it, Clarissa, that you are betrothed to the absent Kit?"

Clarissa's expression clouded. "We have exchanged vows, which is the same thing."

"Not quite," she was told gently. "And certainly not in the eyes of the world."

"What it is to have a perfidious guardian! Hugo is cruel and harsh, without a thought for my feelings!" Tugging her bonnet strings undone, she hurled that dashing object onto the bed and sank down beside it, bursting into tears. "Only think, my poor Kit is about to return to the Peninsula and my hateful brother orders me to receive the attentions of a suitor!"

"That does sound a little insensitive, to be sure,"

observed Miss Standish, perceiving the very real unhappiness of the sobbing girl. A knock at the door proclaimed the arrival of the tea tray, and after taking it herself, she poured a cup and persuaded her companion to take a few comforting sips.

"With the privilege allowed to a proxy aunt, may I ask if this Kit of yours is a suitable match?" she asked delicately.

Clarissa sniffed dolefully. "How can he not be, when we played together as children?" she asked. "He is brave and dashing. General Wellington praised him, you know, for his part in the battle of Vitoria, but he is poor and has his own way to make in the world. When I have an *enormous* fortune, it is ridiculous that I am not allowed to share it with him."

"Forgive me, but aren't you a little young to have control of it?"

Clarissa sent her a speaking look. "I inherit when I am one and twenty—or upon my marriage, but only if Hugo approves of my match!"

"I see."

"It is the most odious thing! How could Julian, who was my guardian after Papa died, have allowed such a clause? To put me completely under the power of a stepbrother whom one can only describe as totally toplofty and obnoxious!"

"Julian?" Miss Standish repeated the name on a questioning note.

"My brother," Clarissa supplied, "and the dearest of men. The fates were unkind to him." Her voice quavered and a large tear trickled down her cheek. "He contracted a disastrous marriage with an actress—and th-then was killed at Talavera."

9

Amy Standish was silent, gazing down into the depths of her teacup with a closed expression on her face. After a long pause, she looked up and found Clarissa's eyes fixed on her. Summoning a rather strained smile to her lips, Amy asked briskly: "What now? Surely you have not run out of plans. I am sadly disappointed in your ingenuity, if you are at a loss."

The sparkling tears were whisked away and Miss Dysart straightened her slim shoulders with decision. "I have been giving the matter my thoughts," she confessed, "and have hit upon a capital plan. With *you* to accompany me—for who could object to so respectable a chaperon as an aunt?—no one could question our traveling on. I am persuaded that Carley Weston is only a few miles distant. I daresay we could be there for dinner, if only we could hire a chaise without that wretched Lucius being aware of our plans."

"If it were only the weather deterring us, for I assure you that the thought of spending the night in a snowdrift does not affect me at all, I should agree. But, flattered as I am that you wish to involve me in your plans, Clarissa dear, I must remind you that I am not, in truth, your aunt and have my own obligations to meet."

Clarissa widened her eyes. "I daresay you were about to take up a governess post with some horrid spoiled brat and some nasty family who would overwork or ignore you," she remarked, with devastating accuracy.

"I am afraid that you are probably right," Miss Standish agreed quietly. "Nevertheless, I have accepted the position and must—"

"Pooh! If you don't arrive, they will just advertise

again. I'll lay odds that you were expecting to be met and that they forgot," Clarissa stated positively. Seeing her companion still obdurate, she became more cunning. "I *shall* go on, you know," she told her. "Only think of the ills that could befall a young and innocent female alone on the roads. Why, I might meet a highwayman—or be abducted by some rogue!" She smiled winningly at the other woman. "Say you'll stay with me, dearest Aunt," she begged, "and we can set off at once."

Miss Standish abandoned her new employers who, as Clarissa had rightly surmised, had not kept their promise to meet the stagecoach, without a qualm; besides, the coincidence of this meeting seemed too opportune not to be used. The name Dysart was too unusual not to be the same, and when twinned with a Julian who had been killed on the Peninsula, the chances of it being a different person were unlikely, to say the least. For five years she and her mother had longed for news of Chloe's child and now this chance meeting held hope that their wish was within possibility. Miss Standish abandoned her principles for the first time in her life, quieting her conscience with the thought that she could make her identity known later, and nodded her agreement.

"Very well, Clarissa—though doubtless I shall regret it when I discover that Mrs. Tompkins is an ideal employer, with a very creditable son on the lookout for a drab female for a wife! However, I collect that you expect the arrival of Sir Hugo at any moment; surely he will not be taken in by your explanation of our kinship."

"No, indeed. *Nothing* will take Hugo in. Just one of his looks and one confesses to anything! The

11

most elaborate story is quite forgot, however well prepared. One can never give the lie to Brother Hugo." She spoke with some rancor and brooded silently for a moment on past injustices before declaring firmly: "There is nothing for it but to find a vehicle and press on. I don't precisely know, but I am persuaded that Carley Weston cannot be far. We *must* reach it—even Hugo would be hard put to snatch me out of Mrs. Masters's house, if I declined to go."

She spoke bravely, but Miss Standish could detect a degree of nervous uncertainty tinged with fear behind her declaration and, remembering the ease with which Sir Hugo Dysart had dealt with her own sister, felt that her previously formed, far-from-favorable opinion of the baron's character was thoroughly vindicated.

As if to confirm her views, Clarissa burst into impassioned speech. "You have no idea how odious he is! Dear Julian was the best of brothers, always ready to dip into his pocket or help one out of scrapes, but *Hugo*—" She spoke the name with dislike. "Hugo is a hard-hearted brute! Everyone must jump to his tune—and all because he had to sell out of the army when Papa died and cut back and scrimp in the most horrid manner to put the estate back on its feet after dear Papa's excesses."

"Forgive me, but how is this?" Amy asked delicately. "I believe that you said you are an heiress."

"Mama's money," was the succinct explanation. "Hugo inherited the estate of Candover Magna, which Papa had allowed to become run-down. He was a gambler, you know," she confided. "When he married Mama as his second wife, her capital was contracted upon her children; poor Papa only had

12

access to the interest. So Julian inherited an estate from Grandpapa Greenhaven, who made his money in the City, and I will be as rich as Croesus when I come of age. Julian said it is unfair and that it was the effort of bringing his inheritance about that made Hugo as mad as a crab." She considered the matter momentarily. "Though why that should make him so—so hard-hearted and cruel, I do not know. I truly believe that his sole ambition is to make m-me miserable and r-run my life in the most odious way!"

"That does seem a little unlikely. From what you tell me, Sir Hugo appears to have little time for such pleasures."

"You do not know him," cried Miss Dysart in tragic tones and would have elaborated upon her stepbrother's perfidious character had she not been interrupted by the arrival of the kettle. Abandoning his lordship, she began to question the landlord's daughter about the possibility of journeying to Carley Weston that day.

"Why, that be all of twelve miles away, miss!" the girl exclaimed, as if it were the moon. "You'll never get there today. There be a cart agoing in that direction tomorrow—if the weather don't close down like. Father reckons we'm in for a blizzard."

Having spent some moments deep in thought while the girl set down the kettle, Clarissa jumped to her feet as soon as she and Amy were alone. "There is nothing for it but to persuade Lucius to allow us to take the chaise as soon as the horses are rested," she declared. "I don't for one moment believe that he was only funning about Gretna as he claims. There was something in his manner that made me uneasy." She shivered slightly at the recollection. "But with you here, I am convinced that he cannot refuse—" Her face suddenly fell. "Unless the vile wretch decided to curry favor with Hugo, which, now that I think of it, is just what he would do. Oh, Aunt Almeria, what *shall* we do?" she cried, her lower lip trembling and her huge eyes filling with brilliant tears that in no way curtailed her beauty.

Miss Standish watched in admiration, never having seen the art of crying brought to such perfection. "Pray tell me how that is done," she said. "It must be of the greatest use."

Clarissa blinked and the tears fell in sparkling drops as she gave a reluctant laugh. "I just think sad thoughts," she said; "though in truth, my thoughts are sad at the moment. Usually it's extremely easy. I've been able to do it since I was a child. It *infuriates* Hugo!"

"I can imagine," returned her companion.

"But what shall we do?" asked the girl, returning to the only matter that interested her.

Amy Standish was saved from the need to reply by the sounds of an approaching vehicle driven at speed. Both ladies listened as the horses were checked and the carriage clearly swung under the arch and was brought to a halt in the yard.

Clarissa turned pale. "Hugo!" she breathed. Her eyes wide with apprehension, she held out an appealing hand to the other woman.

Miss Standish, who had suspected that Clarissa's fear of Sir Hugo was mainly playacting, saw that she was genuinely frightened and moved quickly to take her hand. "I am sure you have nothing to fear," she said reassuringly. "Be calm—

14

your brother is not likely to create a scene. Gentlemen do not care for them, you know."

"Oh, you are not aware—" the girl whispered. "He has threatened to send me to a school in the remotest countryside where I should never see my dearest Kit again. Hugo can look so . . . It makes one wish to die!"

The ladies listened to the sound of Hugo's arrival below, clearly recognizing Mr. Gambrill's rather petulant tones raised in greeting and then the closing of a door as the gentlemen obviously retired to talk in private.

"I should have known that Lucius could be so traitorous," was Clarissa's comment.

Miss Standish looked at her curiously. "What will he tell your brother? How will he explain his presence? Will Sir Hugo believe his tale of pretending to take flight for Scotland in order to frighten you?"

"At the time *I* believed him; he seemed quite wicked, but now . . . it seems rather a harebrained notion. I only had a few essentials in a carpetbag and he had nothing! I daresay it would be like him to frighten me in order to put himself in favor with Hugo."

The door behind them opened and the landlord's daughter appeared once more. "Sir Hugo would be obliged if Miss Dysart would favor him with her presence," she enunciated carefully, obviously delivering a well-prepared speech.

Clarissa gasped and clutched her companion's hand. "Come with me," she begged.

"Remember, I am a stranger to him—he will feel that I intrude," Amy protested.

"I cannot—*will* not go alone," the girl declared,

15

looking ready to faint. "Please, oh, *please* give me your support," she pleaded. "You cannot desert me now! I count on you as a friend!"

Her distress aroused Miss Standish's sympathy and she agreed reluctantly, adding as calmly as she could, "Compose yourself—I've always found that gentlemen have a ready dislike of hysterics. Indeed, a nervous spasm invariably serves to arouse their annoyance, which is the very last thing you must wish to do."

Clarissa acknowledged the sense of this advice and struggled to calm herself with praiseworthy effort. It was only the slight trembling of her hands that betrayed the agitation she felt as she advanced bravely into the room to confront the man awaiting her.

"H-Hugo," she said with a catch of her breath that would have softened the hardest heart.

The tall man, who had been deep in conversation with Lucius Gambrill, turned as she spoke and surveyed her coldly. Miss Standish, who still stood in the open doorway, took note of the drab-colored driving coat opened and thrown carelessly back over broad shoulders, displaying a blue cutaway jacket and buff buckskin breeches tucked into gleaming Hessians. Only once she had taken in the full elegance of his attire did she raise her eyes to study the face above the snowy folds of the neckcloth. She had an impression of an aquiline nose above a rather hard mouth and hair so dark a red that it resembled mahogany, before she became aware that she, herself, was the object of scrutiny by a pair of curiously dark gray eyes.

"Cousin Almeria, I presume," Sir Hugo said,

coming forward with his hand held out. "What a surprise to meet you here."

There was nothing for it but to give him her hand and summon a smile. "A coincidence of the first water," she agreed, while Clarissa stood as if turned to stone. Mr. Gambrill, Amy noted, who had watched this scene with ill-concealed interest, appeared decidedly displeased, a frown between his brows as he studied her with a sharp, blue gaze.

"Make your thanks to Lucius, Clarissa, for his kindness in escorting you and let him be on his way," Sir Hugo continued. "The weather threatens to become bad and we all have some miles farther to travel."

"I—do not understand," Clarissa protested faintly, turning imploring eyes toward the other woman.

"The cold must have turned your brain," her brother told her unkindly. "Even you cannot have forgotten that we are to spend some time in the country due to your indisposition! By now all your friends will have been acquainted with the fact. I left Miss Witherspoon penning the notes." He looked at his sister and smiled patronizingly. "You really should have thought of it yourself, Clarissa. I am sure that you would not care to be the talk of the Town!" Her lips opened and closed silently and he turned his attention to his kinsman. "We will keep you no longer, Lucius. I know how eager you are to get back to London."

Mr. Gambrill looked about to protest, but one look into his cousin's formidable face convinced him that such an action would not be wise, and making an attempt to hide his reluctance, he took his leave of the ladies.

17

As he reached the door Sir Hugo's voice stopped him. "And Lucius—remember how unhappy I should be if any adverse tale about today carried to my ears. You need only to make it known that you escorted Clarissa to meet me here, to earn my gratitude."

Remembering the generous allowance his cousin made him, Lucius nodded briefly, and shortly he could be heard shouting for his carriage to be brought round.

"*Now*, Clarissa," began the tall man menacingly, and instinctively the girl shrank away, possessing herself of Miss Standish's hand, which she clung to with desperate fingers.

Recognizing the signs of an approaching attack of hysterics, Miss Standish took positive action. "Now, Clarissa," she repeated, but in quite different tones to those his lordship had used. "I am persuaded that nothing would prove more detrimental to your cause than to behave badly. Gentlemen do *not* care to be submitted to an attack of the vapors. Besides, nothing is so ruinous to one's beauty, you know."

Miss Dysart blinked at her matter-of-fact tone and, struck by the truth of the advice, abandoned the scene she had been about to enact; instead she allowed her eyes to fill with tears and regarded her brother through drenched, sparkling lashes.

"Yes, very effective," he said, greeting this act dryly, "but remember that such wiles are wasted on me. Good God, child, what were you thinking of! Have you no more care for your reputation than to fly to your lover like a Brighton Miss? Thank Heaven that Lucius saw you and had the forethought to accompany you. I had thought better of

18

Kit Masters than that he would encourage you in such madness!"

Clarissa blinked away her tears in order to glare at her brother. "Kit had no idea—he is not even at home. I intended to seek sanctuary with his mother!"

"Seek sanctuary!" repeated Sir Hugo blankly. "I knew those Gothic novels you are forever reading would turn your head. If you think a vicar's wife would agree to keep you from your family, you are even more wanting than I thought. Of all the hen-brained schemes—why would you want to do anything so pea-witted?"

Miss Dysart's chest swelled with indignation. "Because you *ordered* me to accept Sir Simon Lovell's addresses," she cried, and dissolved into loud, hiccuping sobs. "H-how could you be so cruel, when you kn-know that I have given my heart to my dearest K-Kit?"

Sir Hugo looked so murderous that Miss Standish felt called upon to intervene. "Your sister is upset," she pointed out, somewhat unnecessarily, as he took a step toward the sobbing girl. "She has had a tiring day and is in need of rest and refreshment. To scold her now will do no good, you know, and will very likely make her ill. Let me take her to her room and in a little while she will be calmer, I promise."

"You do not know Clarissa," she was told bitterly. Hugo Dysart gave her his full attention and she was aware of being appraised by his cold, gray eyes, which were so dark as to be almost black. Abruptly growing bored with the whole affair, he swung away to stare out of the window. "Very well, Miss Standish, do as you please," he said, drumming his nails on the windowsill. "You may have half an hour, no more."

Amy Standish hurried the girl from the room. "I am surprised that you have not learned to manage your brother better," she commented as they crossed the dark hallway. "I've never known enacting a Cheltenham tragedy to do other than infuriate the male sex."

Clarissa looked back, her hand on the newel post. "I've never thought to manage Hugo," she admitted unhappily. "He is so—so coldhearted that I hold him in dread. He is nearly twenty years older than me, and as a child I hardly saw him—I only heard of his exploits. Then when Papa died and Hugo sold out of the army, he descended upon me like . . . like a *jailer* and declared that I had been allowed to grow out of hand and sent me to a seminary for young ladies that was more like a prison than a school—it was no wonder that I ran away, and to say that Signor Valetti had anything to do with it was quite untrue. He chanced to come upon me in the street and it was the worst of luck that Hugo should happen to choose that very moment to drive down Wickham's high street—just when the signor was comforting me!"

"I—see. It is quite understandable how such a thing could be misconstrued," murmured Amy Standish, following her vocal charge up the stairs. "How very unfortunate."

"It was," agreed the girl, who seemed to have recovered from her indisposition. "Hugo can look very nasty, you know, though I must own to being a little disappointed in the way Signor Valetti *crumbled* under Hugo's tongue-lashing!"

Marching ahead of Amy, she entered their room

and, wetting her handkerchief in the water jug, dabbed at her flushed face. "Well, Aunt Almeria," she said, a faint tremor in her voice. "What do we do now?"

Amy looked at her kindly, seeing the very real unhappiness on the young face. "I do not believe that I have anything to do with it," she pointed out gently.

The girl's face crumpled and the ready tears appeared again. "Oh, please!" she cried. "I thought it was all arranged. I need you!"

"You seem to have forgot that I am not really your aunt," Amy reminded her. "For his own reasons, Sir Hugo allowed Mr. Gambrill to believe so, but he, of all people, must be aware that I am not related."

Clarissa seemed much struck by this. "I wonder why?"

"I daresay he did not wish to put you to the blush—"

"Pooh! Little you know Hugo," retorted Clarissa with a return of spirit. "He would positively relish seeing my confusion." She paused, biting her lip and eyeing her companion from under thick lashes. "Could you not be persuaded to become my companion, *dearest* honorary Aunt?" she wheedled. "I would be good with you, I promise I would. Only think how that would please my brother. Withy— Miss Witherspoon, who was my governess until Hugo sent me off to school and whom he reinstated when—when I had to leave, is the kindest creature, but so timid and circumspect, always expecting the worst of me, that I must confess she brings out the very worst in my nature. She *twitters*—and flutters until I find I am set upon doing the very thing that

21

has thrown her into a nervous spasm in the first place." Clasping her hands under her chin in an appealing gesture, she entreated: "Oh, pray say you will do as I ask."

Miss Standish felt she could readily understand such feelings, having found herself much irritated by flustered gentility. Nevertheless, she shook her head. "My dear, I can hardly put myself forward in such a way—it would not be proper and Sir Hugo would be very right in deciding that I was too coming by half. Neither he nor you know anything about me—"

Before Clarissa could reply, the maidservant put her head round the door to inform them that the gentleman wanted Miss Standish to join him in the parlor, and she volunteered the information that he wasn't in a pretty temper, neither.

The two women exchanged startled glances; neither was quite ready for such a move, thinking that they had time to compose themselves. Clarissa gasped and sank down upon the bed, her face so white and despairing that Amy Standish was filled with compassion.

"Don't look like that," she cried involuntarily, and found herself promising to do her best on the other's behalf; though how and in what way, she had no very clear idea.

CHAPTER TWO

Sir Hugo Dysart turned from the window as she entered and, taking up his quizzing glass, surveyed her through the small, round lens, his gray gaze decidedly severe and autocratic. Refusing to allow herself to be intimidated, Miss Standish returned his gaze with a lift of her eyebrows before she crossed to the fire and seated herself composedly, folding her hands neatly in her lap.

"I am sure you can have no idea of the alarm with which your sister regards you," she began conversationally. "The poor child is convinced that you intend to marry her off out of hand to a bridegroom to whom she has taken an aversion, which of course has only served to convince her all the more of her enduring love for her childhood friend." Looking at the driving coat he had discarded over the back of a chair, she noticed the whip ends threaded through a buttonhole and commented dryly: "I am persuaded that you would not treat a spirited horse so harshly."

Black eyebrows drew together as he ignored her question. "And who, madam, are you . . . precisely?" he asked dangerously.

"I, sir, am The Only Hope," Miss Standish told him and saw one eyebrow fly up. Knowing that she

23

had caught his attention, she continued: "As she was in some distress, Clarissa saw me as a savior and asked for my help. To be *precise*, I am Amy Standish." Watching closely, she saw that the name meant nothing to him.

Barely acknowledging her introduction, Sir Hugo regarded her steadily with narrowed eyes and returned to the subject that interested him. "Why should Clarissa be in distress?" he asked.

"Perhaps she has not had a chance to tell you— though I am not sure that she would, as she seems to regard you with a degree of nervousness. The truth of the matter is that when she arrived here, she believed that Mr. Gambrill was carrying her off to Gretna!"

"Nonsense," his lordship said firmly.

"No, it is not nonsense," Miss Standish returned. "Whether you believe that abduction was his intention or not, the fact is that Clarissa was frightened enough to seek aid from a stranger, and even if Mr. Gambrill's only intention was to teach her a lesson, as he later informed her, surely her discipline is a matter for her guardian and no one else."

"He told me only that Clarissa behaved like a tragedy queen, and knowing my sister's propensity for drama, I could well believe him. Indeed, if I had not heard this tale from you, I would have thought she was embroidering matters in her usual fashion."

The stern look had softened slightly but the embers of anger still gleamed in the back of his eyes as he studied her. Not liking the shrewd examination, Amy Standish looked away, turning her face into the shadows. She had intended making herself known to him, but confronted by Sir Hugo's formidable presence, she found that her courage deserted her and she could not bring herself to announce her relationship to his dead brother's despised wife; instead she decided to satisfy her conscience by doing what she could for Clarissa, who undoubtedly stood in need of a friend. "Your sister, sir, may be inclined to melodrama, but she is a very unhappy girl. I believe that she would be better managed by kindness and understanding than the harsh methods now employed—"

"Oh, do you, Miss—" Breaking off, he searched for her name in vain. "I have forgot your name, pray enlighten me," he said briefly.

"Standish," she supplied, knowing that the name meant nothing to him, as Chloe had lost no time abandoning it for something more impressive and fanciful when she went upon the stage.

"Well then, Miss Standish—" he began menacingly, but then, recollecting the impropriety of discussing his sister's life with a stranger, he made her a frosty bow. "Allow me to express my gratitude for your aid."

"You must admit that your methods haven't worked too well," she observed mildly. "You are irritated by her and she is afraid of you!"

He had been about to give her a set-down, but his expression changed at her last words. "Afraid!" he repeated.

"Yes. She believes that now you will incarcerate her in some remote seminary for rebellious females." Watching his face, she recognized various fleeting emotions, from surprise to chagrin, and surprised herself by saying quietly: "I believe that I could manage her—"

"Touting for business?" he asked sharply, making

25

her raise startled eyes to his face. What he saw in her expression made him ask another question. "What do you mean?" he demanded in a different tone.

"I—scarcely know. Indeed, I have no idea why I said that, except that I think that I could manage her . . . and that she is truly unhappy."

"And that you believe her tales of being badly treated. Let me make it quite plain that she has never wanted for anything. She has been much indulged and *that*, Miss Standish, and not my attempts to rectify her character, is the cause of any unhappiness she might feel. She is a spoiled minx who needs to learn how to control her wild behavior before she is let free on the world."

"You are right," Amy agreed, "but having failed with harsh measures, would it not be wiser to try something kinder?"

Sir Hugo regarded her cynically. "I suppose you are about to offer your services," he observed with a curl of his lip.

Amy nodded with a composure she was far from feeling. "Yes," she said simply. "A spirited girl, almost of an age to come out, needs other than her childhood governess—who, while no doubt suited to the care of a child, has not the experience to deal with a lively, difficult young female, almost of an age to embark upon her first Season."

"And you could?"

"I am prepared to try. Clarissa has already suggested that I become her companion. Indeed, she has promised to be on her best behavior if I can persuade you to agree."

"Indeed!" He gave a harsh bark of laughter. "I

26

am not used to being presented with a fait accompli."

There was silence while he examined the woman before him, and Amy bore his scrutiny with a degree of aplomb. Sir Hugo saw a woman out of the first flush of youth, with a neat figure and soft mouse-colored hair arranged in a rather severe plaited coronet. Her donkey-brown gown and black spencer jacket were quietly elegant, the severity of her outfit softened by a frill of lace at the throat. A pair of small, wire-framed spectacles perched on her nose, detracting from her attractive features, and only when she looked up was it apparent that her eyes were an unexpected shade of hazel.

"Do I know you? You seem familiar," Sir Hugo said abruptly.

A hint of color appeared in Miss Standish's normally rather pale cheeks, but she answered calmly in the negative. "As far as I am aware, we have never met, sir," she said truthfully.

He frowned, but appeared satisfied. "Do you have references?" he asked curtly, and Amy reached into her reticule and produced some folded sheets of paper.

"I'll leave you to peruse them," she suggested.

"Send Clarissa to me," Sir Hugo instructed, not turning from the window where he had retired to read the closely written pages.

"Your brother would like to see you," Amy told the wide-eyed girl, who looked up hopefully at her entrance.

"He has agreed! Oh, *dear* Aunt Almeria, how clever you are," she cried, jumping to her feet and dropping an impulsive kiss on Amy's cheek before she ran from the room.

27

Once alone, Amy crossed to the spotted mirror that hung above the shallow washing bowl and peered into its yellow depths. "Oh, how could you be so perfidious?" she breathed, removing the disfiguring spectacles and staring at her reflection. "How can you hope to deceive him?" Reading the resolution reflected in her green eyes, she knew that the thought of her mother's joy at hearing news of her grandson, Penn, would make her action worthwhile, and squaring her shoulders, she gave a little nod of determination. "After all, Sir Hugo is in the wrong with his arrogant disregard for Mama's feelings," she told herself. "Of course, Chloe was wrong to agree that Penn should be given entirely into the Dysarts' care . . . but for Sir Hugo to insist that we have no contact whatsoever with him cannot be considered anything other than unreasonably harsh and autocratic."

Her pensive thoughts were disturbed by the sound of rapidly approaching footsteps and she just had time to replace her spectacles as Clarissa danced into the room.

"How did you contrive it?" she cried, her face aglow. "How clever you must be, dearest Aunt! Hugo only read me the most mild of scolds and even suggested that he may have been in the wrong to put me in the care of Withy and proposed that if I gave my word to be good, he would offer you the post of my companion! I cannot believe such luck, for it is the thing that I most desire. He even seemed a little averse to Lucius, whom you must know is the biggest toadeater and sets himself out to please anyone with money or position."

Miss Standish's heart gave a violent thump against her spencer as she realized that she was committed to a life of deception, and for one wild moment she considered making good her escape, but a glance at Clarissa's bright countenance and hopeful eyes made her aware of new and previously unconsidered responsibilities. The moment of panic passed and she became aware that her companion was chatting.

"Hugo says that the weather is too bad for us to travel on in his curricle and that he has sent Tedbury, his groom, on to the Manor to bring his chaise over in the morning." She gave a sudden gurgle of laughter. "Hugo has not completely reformed, for he says that the journey will be deuced uncomfortable and that I have only myself to blame!"

Sir Hugo's newfound amiability did not extend to dining with the two ladies; their meal was served in their bedroom, while Clarissa's brother ate in the parlor. By morning the snow had ceased to fall and Amy awoke to an unexpected brightness filling the room. Crossing the cold wooden floor on bare feet to peer out of the latticed window, she was greeted by a uniform white world. Trails of wheel marks and footprints in the yard indicated that someone was already about, and a few strands of smoke rising from nearby chimneys spoke of village folk stirring. Behind her, footsteps clattered up the stairs and Bessie appeared in the doorway carrying kindling and an armful of logs.

Seeing Amy by the window in her nightdress, she clicked her tongue. "You'll catch your death, miss," she reproved her. "Just you hop back in bed until I've lit the fire. There's no need for you to be up and about at this hour, even if his lordship is on the prowl."

As soon as she had gone, Amy hurriedly washed and dressed beside the meager warmth of the newly lit fire and, by the time a sleepy Clarissa was stirring, was ready to leave the room.

"I believe that Sir Hugo will wish to make an early start," she reminded her. "Although the snow must be a foot deep, the sky is clear and some wheeled vehicle has already been about the yard."

Clarissa turned over and snuggled deeper under the blankets. "*Dear* Aunt Almeria," she wheedled, "pray ask for my breakfast to be brought up."

"Slugabed! Very well, but only if you promise to be quick. I feel it would not be wise to strain Sir Hugo's patience."

Descending the stairs, Miss Standish met that gentleman coming in from the yard. He brought a cloud of freezing air with him and she involuntarily shivered.

"Yes, it is extremely cold," he commented, holding the parlor door for her. "However, Tedbury has just arrived and reports that the roads are passable." Noticing Clarissa's absence, he added: "I trust that my sister is astir."

"I have her promise to be down shortly," she assured him, and somewhat to their surprise, Miss Dysart kept her word, appearing just as Amy was finishing her coffee, looking ravishing in her modish bonnet and pelisse of rose pink velvet.

"You are looking very fetching," commented Sir Hugo, smiling lazily.

The compliment obviously surprised her, for her eyes opened wide and her cheeks flushed to match her outfit. "Are you roasting me?" she demanded.

"No—just setting you up to be amenable to wearing the cloak Tedbury has brought with him," her

30

brother told her, a hint of amusement in his eyes. "I am aware that it will spoil the effect of your ensemble, but no one but I will see it, and for once I insist that you put sense before fashion."

"Only think how inconvenient it would be if you took a chill and had to spend days in your bedchamber," put in Miss Standish on seeing the slender shoulders stiffen.

Recognizing his mistake, Sir Hugo tipped up his sister's mutinous chin and smiled down into her stormy eyes. "Don't be forever at odds with me," he advised. "I meant nothing more than your welfare—the cold is bitter and you will be glad of whatever warmth there is. You know there is nothing so icy as a carriage in winter."

Rather to her surprise, Amy Standish found that she, too, had been provided with a thick woolen cloak, and well-wrapped against the inclement weather and with hot bricks at their feet, the ladies set out on their journey with a sense of adventure.

John Tedbury drove the coach while Sir Hugo rode ahead on his black gelding, and the groom who had brought it over from Candover Magna that morning rode alongside. At first, despite the thick snow, the journey was fairly easy, but once the main road was left behind, the way became more difficult.

After a particularly violent jolt, caused by a deep, hidden rut, Sir Hugo appeared at the window of the coach. "Don't scowl at me, miss," he told Clarissa cheerfully, having made sure that they had not suffered any hurt. "You have yourself to thank for any discomfort. If you had not chosen to act the part of one of the mutton-headed heroines you are always reading about, you would be sitting

31

cozily beside the fire, discussing your latest conquest with one of your cronies."

"Mutton-headed!" repeated Clarissa as he rode ahead again, "of all the things! I am sure they behave with great sensibility, which no one could accuse my odious brother of having." She turned to Miss Standish. "I am persuaded that you must enjoy a novel."

"Indeed, yes," Amy agreed readily. "Jane Austen is a great favorite."

"I find her books too ordinary by half," Clarissa admitted. "It's like reading an account of one's own life. I prefer something more exciting. Mrs. Radcliffe is a little old-fashioned now, but Mr. Maturin can make one's blood run cold in the most frightful manner. There can be nothing nicer than to read *The Fatal Revenge* while tucked up in bed, with the howling wind making the candles flicker in a delightfully spine-chilling way."

The ladies fell into a discussion of their favorite authors while the miles passed slowly, and it was not until some time later that Clarissa became aware that the bricks on which their feet rested were no longer hot and that an insidious chill was creeping into the chaise. Winding down the window and letting in a blast of icy air, she called imperiously to her brother, making her discomfort clear.

Sir Hugo handed in his hip flask at the window. "Clary," he said wearily, using her childhood name, "do not be making a fuss, I beg. I cannot procure a fire or a hot meal out of thin air. Neither can I make the snow miraculously disappear, as even you must be aware. Wrap yourself in the rugs—we have only a few miles to travel now. We'll be home in no time."

Miss Standish suspected that he was misleading his sister and, indeed, "a few miles" proved to be an understatement, for the thin winter sun was beginning to set and the shadows to lengthen as the procession finally left the road and drove between a pair of high pillars, past a lodge-house, and along a tree-lined drive. Clarissa regained her spirits and emerged from her fur nest, eagerly pointing out the exact moment when the Manor would come into view.

"There!" she cried excitedly. "Is it not beautiful? I vow I had forgot how welcoming and attractive it is."

And indeed, Candover Magna was a perfect example of an old-fashioned redbrick manor house. Built sometime before the Civil War, the rose red house sat snugly on a slight rise in the ground, columns of blue smoke rising lazily from its twisting chimneys. The low, winter sun struck like gold on the latticed panes of glass in the mullioned windows, making an unexpectedly colorful scene of one that should, by rights, have been all drab gray and cold white.

The coach swung around in front of the house and drew to a halt beside the front door, which had been flung open at the first sound of their approaching wheels. A small, rotund man stood on the shallow steps, beaming and bowing a welcome, as the chaise door was opened and the steps lowered.

"Sir Hugo, Miss Clary—how good to see you!" he said, any inconvenience to him in what he expected would be leisurely winter months obviously forgotten in his pleasure at having the family at home.

"Well, Hill, how are you and Mrs. Hill?" asked

33

Sir Hugo easily, swinging down from his saddle and giving his mount into the care of a stable boy who had run out from the back of the house.

The ladies had already hurried into the hall and Sir Hugo followed them. Putting back his driving coat, he handed his hat and gloves to a hovering footman and joined his sister and Miss Standish who were standing in front of the blazing logs that filled the great stone fireplace at one end of the hall.

A large, but equally rotund, woman appeared bearing a tray. "Welcome, my lord—miss," she said, putting her burden down on a table near the fire. "I thought the ladies would welcome a cup of tea," she said, "but perhaps you would care for something stronger, sir?"

"Tea would be very pleasant as long as it is accompanied by a slice of your fruitcake," Sir Hugo told her, to her pleasure, slipping out of his caped coat. "Let me introduce Miss Standish who is my sister's new companion," he went on, turning to Amy to add: "The Hills were here when I was born, though not in the capacity of butler and housekeeper."

"No, my lord—I was under-footman and Mary was just starting as upper-housemaid. Just young things, we were, starting out in life."

Sir Hugo clapped the older man on the shoulder in a friendly fashion. "Where would we be without you both to keep an eye on the Manor," he wondered aloud as Mrs. Hill poured the tea, having settled the ladies in chairs where they could thaw their frozen feet by the heat of the fire.

"And Penn, how is he?" inquired Sir Hugo, looking round as if expecting to see his nephew. "I should have thought he would have been here before now."

"Master Penn is abed—Miss James having decided he was likely to have taken a chill while snowballing yesterday."

There was a note of underlying disapproval in her voice and Amy, who had been careful to show no particular interest at the mention of her nephew's name, looked up to surreptitiously study the housekeeper's impassive countenance. Sir Hugo's eyebrows rose, but he made no comment beyond remarking that he would go up and see the boy shortly.

"Miss Standish is in the Blue Room," Mrs. Hill told Clarissa as she escorted the ladies upstairs.

Clarissa's brows rose expressively. "You must have pleased Hugo," she confided. "The long corridor is usually reserved for family. We are all there—Hugo, by the stairs in the Cavalier Room, which is the master bedroom; Julian's old room is next. I have the room in the middle, and the Blue Room is opposite it, at the far end. You have a view across the grounds toward the village, hidden behind a belt of trees. Only the tower of St. Thomas's church shows above them."

"And where is Penn?" Amy could not forbear asking.

"He's safe in the nursery wing—you need have no fear that he will disturb you," she was told. "Indeed, he rarely disturbs anyone. His health is not good, you know."

"No, I did not know," said Amy slowly. "Is it anything serious?"

Clarissa was undecided. "I don't think so—it seems to have happened in the last few years. He was a robust baby. I remember being much impressed by his roars of disapproval when he exchanged his dearly loved wet nurse for Miss James and Nanny Brown."

She left her companion at her door, promising to return to escort her downstairs to dinner, which would be at the country hour of six, instead of the fashionably late hour kept in Town.

Left to herself, Amy Standish looked around, noting the blue brocade at the windows and the blue embroidered hanging over the bed that obviously gave the room its name. A coal fire burned in the hearth, its flickering flames reflected on the dark, paneled walls and wide, polished floorboards. A worn Chinese rug covered part of the floor and a tall Georgian armchair waited invitingly near the fire. The furniture spoke more of comfort than fashion, and she was momentarily surprised that it had not been replaced with something more elegant, until she recalled that this was the Dysarts' country home and so did not need to reflect their wealth and position in society.

Amy's small, much-worn trunk was brought up, and after helping her unpack and put away her clothes, a maid bore away her slate-blue crepe evening gown to remove the creases, leaving her to remove the signs of travel and rest before the gong sounded for dinner.

Later, dressed in the dull crepe, Amy surveyed herself in a looking glass. The high-necked, long-sleeved gown was simple enough in style to be quietly elegant, but her heart pined for a prettier color that would set off her coloring; the necessity of dressing in the retiring fashion befitting a governess was a sore trial, she had discovered long ago.

Shortly after she became a governess, the need to camouflage her youth and attractive features had been borne upon her. Having studied her somber reflection in a searching manner, she selected a little lace cap and pinned it to the severe plaited coronet that crowned her head and, after a moment's reflection, replaced her spectacles and then sat quietly in the large armchair until Clarissa tapped at the door.

"A cap!" she commented incredulously, coming into the room. "It makes you look twice your age!"

Amy refrained from remarking that that was its precise purpose, instead pointing out mildly that she felt it obligatory wear for an aunt.

"Fudge!" cried Clarissa. "Aunt Augusta never wears such a thing, and she would be of an age with Grandpapa!"

"I collect that she must be on your father's side," mused Miss Standish dryly, causing her companion to give an appreciative gurgle of laughter.

Amy found herself the recipient of Sir Hugo's sharp gaze as the ladies entered the dining room, and she felt, uncomfortably, that he had noticed the mended tear in her elbow-shawl and undoubtedly was aware of the age of her one and only evening gown. His glance lingered a moment on her cap and she was almost sure that his eyebrows twitched slightly as he came forward with impeccable manners to lead them to their seats at the long table.

The meal proceeded pleasantly until the table was cleared and the servants left the room, having replaced the dessert dishes with bowls of nuts and fruits. Looking up from quartering an apple, Sir Hugo eyed his sister, who was in the act of snipping a few grapes from a bunch that hung over the fruit bowl in an artistic manner.

"Clarissa, my dear," he began, "you may be sure that I have noted your new lightness of mood, and while welcoming it, I do wonder a little at its cause."

Amy, who had been puzzled by the same thing, turned to look at the young girl opposite her. She was sitting very upright, the silver scissors held aloft, betraying points of color flaring in her cheeks.

"Can it be, I wonder, that you have recalled that Carley Weston is only ten miles distant? If so, my dear sister, I feel that I must point out that any clandestine communication between our houses will earn my greatest displeasure, and any servant so foolish as to carry a missive from you will be instantly dismissed."

The scissors were flung down on the table with a sharp snap as Clarissa eyed her brother stormily. "Am I to regard myself as a prisoner?" she demanded, red with anger. "Are you ordering me to cut my acquaintance with the Masters? Which you must know would be the most uncivil thing as well as being thought too toplofty by far!"

"Don't be ridiculous," she was told curtly. "You know very well that the Masters are numbered among our friends." Sir Hugo paused, his gray eyes stern. "And that, Clarissa, is how I wish them to remain. Any correspondence between us will be between Mrs. Masters and myself. Do you understand?"

"Oh, I understand very well," she returned ominously. "I understand that you intend to break my heart! That nothing matters to you save wealth and position. That your own h-heart is so cold and unfeeling that you have no idea of how it feels to l-love someone!" She dashed away the angry tears and regarded Sir Hugo, her bosom heaving with emotion. "How could you be so cruel—so *small-minded*? I *love* Kit! You may lock me in my room and st-starve me—I shall never marry the old bridegroom you have selected for me!"

For a moment she looked as if she would seize the fruit bowl and hurl it at her brother, but his steady gaze discouraged such an act and after a moment, she gave a final wild sob and ran from the room. The door crashed back against the wall, bouncing on its hinges, leaving Sir Hugo so white with anger that Miss Standish felt called upon to intervene.

"She is very upset—" she began, and his glittering black gaze was turned on her.

"I do not see, Miss Standish, how, with your short acquaintance, you have any knowledge of Clarissa," he remarked coldly.

"No. Indeed, how could I?" she agreed ingenuously. "But I do understand young females. If you recollect from my references, that has been my task for the last seven years."

The tall man studied her and she was momentarily distracted by the way his gray eyes were now so dark as to resemble jet. "Clarissa is wayward and uncontrolled," he said curtly. "She needs a tight rein, which she shall have until she learns to accept what is best for her."

"Ah! But then, you see, she will undoubtedly have very differing views about that."

He looked at her narrowly. "Do you expect me to give my consent to her marriage with a penniless

39

boy, scarce older than herself? Good God—a pretty guardian I should be, if I did so!"

"Yes," agreed his companion. "But did she show any urgent desire to be married to Kit until she was presented with the aged suitor of your choice?"

"Aged!" repeated Sir Hugo, incensed. "Sir Simon Lovell can give me a good five years!"

"However ridiculous it may seem to us, at seventeen, someone of one and thirty can appear almost in their dotage, especially when put forward as a husband," Amy pointed out. "I am certain that Clarissa regards anyone over thirty as having one foot, at least, in the grave." She paused before going on. "I am right, am I not, in supposing that she had shown no sign previously of considering herself handfasted?" Sir Hugo nodded thoughtfully and she went on: "May I suggest that, perhaps, the proposition of a suitor was not handled with enough delicacy? Young girls easily take fright, you know."

"To be honest, I do not know how she heard of the possibility—and it was only that. Simon Lovell is eminently suitable, an older brother of an acquaintance of Clarissa's, and, very rightly, he called on me to make his feelings known and to inquire if I would oppose his suit in the future. It was no more than that, I assure you."

"You would do best to assure Clarissa. I fear the damage may be done and Sir Simon's suit irreparably tarnished—it is to be feared that she may hold him in aversion."

"Very likely," he commented dryly. "Having seen Clarissa at her worst, do you still intend to take the post? Or has the wretched girl frightened you off?"

"Not at all," Amy returned with composure, glad to see that his eyes had returned to their normal color and were now merely frosty gray, rather than obsidian black. "I often felt that my mama was very wrong in her dealings with my older sister—" She broke off, wishing that she had not mentioned Chloe, and hurried on: "and since then I have had the care of several young ladies much of an age with Clarissa. I am convinced that to forbid contact with someone only has the effect of making them at once eminently desirable."

Sir Hugo looked grimly amused. "Perhaps. I must admit that my attempts to deal with Clarissa have met with little success. . . . They seem merely to have estranged us. Very well, Miss Standish, within reason, I am prepared to try your methods. Which means we must discuss business. I am prepared to pay you—" and here he mentioned an amount that took Amy Standish's breath away. "As soon as my secretary arrives, I shall ask him to write out a contract, if you are agreeable."

Hiding the astonished delight at his unexpected generosity, she indicated that she was and, accepting her overt dismissal, went to the door, only to be stopped by Sir Hugo's voice.

"Miss Standish—I daresay you have your reasons for wearing those spectacles. Pray accept my assurance that there is no need to blight your appearance here," he said. Startled, she looked over her shoulder to find herself apparently dismissed and forgotten about as the baronet gave all his attention to refilling his glass.

41

CHAPTER THREE

Amy woke the next morning to a steady sound of dripping and at first thought that the roof must be leaking until, recalling her surroundings, she realized that such an event would be unlikely in Sir Hugo's well-ordered household. Drawing back her curtains, she saw that the thaw had arrived overnight and the snow was rapidly dissolving, creating a wet and dismal world.

The house was already astir, sounds of brisk scurrying feet and the subdued hum of voices telling of servants setting the rooms to rights and clearing and lighting fires. Peering out into the gray half-dawn, she was startled by a sudden slither and thud as a fold of snow left the roof and fell past her window. Dark patches were appearing on the lawn like holes in a tablecloth and she knew that shortly the roads would be clear and traffic able to move once more.

Amy breakfasted in lonely splendor, Clarissa having sent word that she would break her fast in bed and Sir Hugo obviously having eaten and gone long since. Even the unusual luxury of eating at leisure, warmed by a blazing fire, palled after a while, and having swallowed her second cup of coffee, Miss Standish went in search of her charge.

She found Clarissa sitting up in bed, wrapped in a soft woolen shawl, morosely nibbling a piece of toast, while a girl scarcely older than herself emptied presses and drawers in an attempt to find something her mistress felt inclined to wear.

"Good Heavens!" exclaimed Amy Standish, raising her eyebrows at the clothes that were draped across the bed, laid over the chairs, and even tossed onto the wide windowseat. "Have you decided to set up shop?"

The girl regarded her gloomily. "I cannot find anything to wear," she complained, a hint of petulance in her voice. She kicked at the pile on the foot of the bed, dislodging several gowns and a blue velvet spencer jacket, which fell to the floor. "There is nothing—*nothing* in which I wish to be seen! These are so old—I took all the best to London."

Miss Standish bent to retrieve the blue jacket and shook out its soft folds. "Well, I cannot conceive why you do not care for this," she told her roundly. "The cornflower blue is so pretty and just the thing to bring out the color of your eyes. Surely there is something to go with it?" She looked around and picked out a round gown in soft cream merino. "This is just the thing, if we take off these ribbons." Pulling them from their casing, she viewed them critically. "Now, in this instance, I do agree with you, Clarissa. What *can* have persuaded you to invest in such a particularly violent shade of puce, which only a gaby could have thought would suit your coloring?"

A reluctant giggle came from the occupant of the bed. "They were all the thing among the girls at school," she admitted, laughing as Amy discarded them with theatrical distaste.

43

Finding a length of blue ribbon, she threaded it through the loops of the dress, while Mary, the maid, entering into the spirit of the thing, declared that she remembered a pair of kid slippers that would just complete the ensemble, if only she could find them. Eventually they were discovered in the bottom of the clothespress, and, much encouraged, Clarissa decided to get up and face the day.

A little later, conscious that she was looking her best, she could face her brother with equanimity when she met him crossing the hall.

"Penn is asking for you," he told her, pausing on the last step of the dogleg stairs. "Miss James seems reluctant to admit visitors, but don't let her put you off; the child needs a distraction." With a cool nod, which included them both, he continued on his way and the study door closed behind him as Clarissa turned to her companion.

"Poor little boy," she said. "I wish I had brought something for him."

"I am sure just seeing a new face will please him." Amy hesitated before speaking again, and when she did so, tried to hide the longing in her voice. "Do you suppose that Sir Hugo would have included me as a distraction?"

Clarissa laughed and seized her hand. "Sure to," she told her, her own spirits quite restored as they climbed the stairs.

The nursery was at the top of the building, on a little landing of its own before the stairs narrowed and continued up to the maids' dormitory. Somewhat to her surprise, for she had been expecting the usual gloomy, ill-equipped rooms, furnished with ancient, rejected furniture, Amy found herself in a white-painted room, with comfortable furnish-

44

ings and a bright fire throwing cozy light on a large rocking horse beside a small cot. As the ladies entered, a soberly dressed woman rose from beside the bed, bending to restrain the occupant who was struggling to sit up and expressing his pleasure at seeing his visitor, in a voice far from that of an invalid.

"Aunt Clary—Aunt Clary! Where have you *been?*"

"London," she said promptly, enfolding him in a hug and kissing him soundly.

Amy was pleased to see the obvious affection between them and, under cover of their chatter, allowed herself to study the nephew she had not seen since he was a baby. Julian Dysart had been as fair as his sister, while Chloe was a ravishing blonde, but Penn's riotous curls owed more to his uncle, having a decidedly red tinge in their dark depths.

"Miss James, how are you?" Clarissa smiled, offering her hand. "Such weather we are having, you may guess what our journey was like. Let me introduce my new companion, Miss Almeria Standish— Penn, this is our Aunt Almeria. Say 'How do you do,' as Miss James has taught you," commanded Clarissa, and Amy, with a shock, found herself being regarded with interest by a pair of eyes as green as her own.

"How do you do," he said obediently, extending his hand. "I'm five," he announced as she took it and gravely bowed.

"I know," she returned, realizing at once that she had betrayed knowledge she should not have. Restraining the urge to gather him into her arms, she added: "I'm very sorry to see that you are unwell."

"I'm *perfectly* well," he said, casting a darkling glance at the silent figure of his governess. "I haven't sneezed once! My nose isn't runny and I haven't coughed—not at *all*!"

"Now, Penn, these ladies will go away if you behave badly," was Miss James's repressive response. "You were feverish yesterday. Mary should never have taken it upon herself to take you out in such bad weather. I have spoken to Sir Hugo about it."

"He won't tell her off! We had fun—Mary's a good girl. We made a snowman . . . and a slide—"

"And got very wet and cold. I will not be responsible if Penn develops a severe chest cold, Miss Clarissa," she added, turning to enlist Clarissa's support. "You know how delicate he is. The least excitement and we have a feverish headache, and I am sorry to say, his chest is not strong."

"I want to get up," her charge put in with every sign of mutiny, his lower lip pouting and his thin black eyebrows drawing together in a frown so reminiscent of his formidable uncle that Amy was hard put to smother a smile.

"I am sure that if you are a good boy, Miss James will allow you to sit by the fire to take your supper, and perhaps your aunt and I could join you for a little while," she put in quickly—though after she had spoken, she grew aware of a disapproving presence beside her.

"I do not think it would be wise," said Honora James coldly, feeling her authority threatened.

"Oh, please say we may," cried Clarissa eagerly. "I am certain it would do no harm, if we don't stay long, and poor little Penn would enjoy it so."

"I am afraid that he will be over excited—"

"We will be as quiet as mice," promised Clarissa

46

with an engaging smile, and taking consent for granted, she turned away to drop a kiss on her nephew's upturned nose. "Now, Penn, be good," she admonished. "Lie quietly abed this afternoon and then Miss James will allow you out of bed later and we will play spillikins after you have eaten all of your supper."

The boy considered the long hours to be endured before his treat but, realizing that nothing would be gained by protesting, murmured agreement. "But I don't care for bread and milk," he pointed out with a baleful glance at a dish of the offending mixture residing on the table beside his bed.

"Then you shan't eat it, my precious!" was his aunt's gratifying response. "You shall have toast and a chicken wing and a cup of hot chocolate."

He beamed at the thought of such a feast but his governess bridled at the slight to her authority. "I do not feel that such rich fare is wise," she asserted.

"Nonsense! Sir Hugo was saying only this morning that Penn needs building up," Clarissa informed her cheerfully. Moving to the mantelpiece, she took down the clock and deposited it on the bedside table. "There. You must lie quietly and do as Miss James tells you and we shall return when the big hand is straight up and the little hand is on the five." With a smile for the governess and a wave to her nephew, she left the room.

Amy followed closely, catching up with her on the landing. "Did Sir Hugo truly say so? I had not thought that you had spoken to him beyond the few minutes in the hall," she said, looking at the younger girl closely.

"No—but I daresay he would have, if he had

thought of it," she retorted. "Poor Penn is looking quite pale and peaked—and if he is being forced to eat bread and milk, which he has always held in the greatest dislike, I am not surprised."

"Miss James does seem rather stern," Amy ventured as they reached the ground floor. "Does Sir Hugo consider him out of hand, too?"

Clarissa gave her a thoughtful look. "Penn is destined for Winchester College, you know. Little boys have need of a stern governess before they are ready for a tutor—if they are to be fit to go away to school at a young age," she said with a matter-of-fact air. "Hugo is well aware of his duties as guardian and as uncle. You may be sure that he has every care for Penn."

"Of course. I should be surprised if he had not," returned Amy, feeling reproved. "It is not my place ... but Miss James seems a little cold toward him. Small children need to be loved—" Unconsciously her voice held a yearning note that made Clarissa glance at her sharply.

"You need have no qualms on that score," Clarissa told her promptly, sounding defensive. "Penn is the most indulged child I know. He will inherit Julian's estate and already thinks himself of great import. I do assure you that everyone is well aware of his position."

Miss Standish thought that this sounded very far from a desirable atmosphere, but said nothing, and Clarissa, who somewhat to her surprise had flown to her brother's defense, changed the subject. Looking out of the window at the dripping scene, she declared that she believed that the roads would be open on the morrow and that above all things she needed to visit the shops in nearby Winchester as soon as possible.

The ladies kept their promise; the resulting games becoming so boisterous that Sir Hugo looked into the nursery to see the cause. Finding Penn and Clarissa noisily encouraging Amy, who was on her knees in the middle of the room, intent upon putting the finishing touch to an enormous card house, he paused in the doorway until it was complete and then startled them all by clapping loudly.

"Well done," he said as Penn hurled himself at his knees.

"Uncle Hugo, Aunt Al—Almy can make *castles* out of cards!"

"So I see," Sir Hugo commented with a lazy smile. "I used to be a dab hand at them, myself." He looked down at Miss Standish, who was in the act of scrambling to her feet. "Are you prepared to take a challenge, Miss Standish?" he asked, extending his hand to her.

Accepting his aid, Amy tried to hide the confusion she felt at being discovered by her employer in such an undignified position. "A challenge?" she repeated, her cheeks burning.

"To make the biggest structure of cards—Penn will be the judge."

"How exciting. A duel!" cried Clarissa, drawing the small boy onto her knee.

"Well?" asked Sir Hugo, still regarding Amy.

"Willingly," she returned. "Though I must warn you, sir, that my talent for such things is prodigious!"

Another pack of cards was produced and the contest begun, both participants taking the affair very seriously. Sir Hugo's structure was bigger and more sturdily built, while Amy's was a delicate effort, appearing to reach for the ceiling in a series of pointed arches. A spirited argument about which was the winner was developing when Miss James returned, her entrance settling the matter by causing the collapse of both edifices. Penn's wail of protest was cut off by his uncle picking him up and depositing him in his cot.

"Behave, brat," he commanded lightly. "Only think what *my* guests would say if I burst into tears when the time came for them to leave!"

This conjured up such a picture of fun that they managed to escape while Penn was still chuckling at the thought of his tearful uncle.

The next day Sir Hugo persuaded Miss James that Penn was fit enough to resume his normal activities, and despite his governess's readily expressed misgivings, when a few days later the ladies decided to drive into Winchester, he was well enough to make known his annoyance at not being included.

"Only think how useful you would be to carry the parcels," Miss Standish remarked. "I daresay you will not mind accompanying us from shop to shop either, and you will only be required to sit quietly while we are actually choosing materials and clothes. I expect we will not spend a *great* deal of time matching ribbons and seeking out hats and gloves. . . ."

Penn rapidly lost interest in the proposed outing and was finally persuaded of the sense of staying home when Amy promised to bring him a surprise.

"To be sure, if you come with us, I could not do so, for *then* it would not be a surprise," she pointed out.

The ladies set out midmorning in the care of Tedbury, intending to lunch at the Red Lion and spend the afternoon indulging in the joys of shopping.

The landlord of the inn greeted Clarissa with the familiarity of one who had known her since childhood. "This is an unexpected pleasure, Miss Clary," he said, leading them into a small, comfortable parlor. "Doubtless you'll be wanting luncheon—there's a nice ham and one of the Missis's fruit pies, just how you like it."

Amy and Clarissa enjoyed their meal and were just about to make their foray into the high street when the landlord interrupted them at the door. "No footman with you, Miss Clary?" he asked, with more than a hint of disapproval.

Clarissa laughed. "In Winchester? Everyone would think I'd grown too toplofty, by far!"

"Well, miss, you be careful. We've had some rough characters about these last few days. Beggars with a very determined way o' begging, if you take my meaning. Won't take no for an answer. The beadle ran 'em out o' town, but I've a feeling that they'll not have gone far, today being Market Day and all."

"We'll take care," Amy assured him, and taking in her quiet air of command and calm manner, he appeared reassured and returned to his other customers.

The little town was busy; townsfolk and people in from the country were taking the opportunity to stock up on necessities in case the weather closed in again. Stalls of produce lined the main street, each stall-holder shouting the name of his wares above the hum of the people who crowded the thor-

51

oughfare. Skirting the noisy throng, Clarissa led the way to her favorite shops and was greeted in each as a valued customer.

Conscious of the quarterly payment Sir Hugo had handed to her that morning, Amy blessed his unexpected forethought, and when she saw a ready-made evening gown displayed invitingly across a table in the modiste's shop, felt able to allow her interest to show.

Madame Jeanne recognized her attention at once and smoothed out an imaginary crease in the clover-colored crepe, saying quietly: "You have the good eye, mademoiselle. Not everyone could wear this color, but you could carry it off to perfection. . . . It was made for a lady, you understand, who then had the alteration of mind and removed herself—I would let it go for the half price. You would like it, no?"

Amy looked again at the elegant cut of the gown, the tight sleeves fastened by tiny pearl buttons, and the bands of deeper-colored velvet edging the slender skirt and was lost, but knew better than to show it. "I am not too sure," she said. "I shall look around, if you please."

Knowing that she had almost certainly made a sale, the Frenchwoman smiled and turned her attention back to Clarissa, who had been pondering the merits of blond silk as well as those of a blush pink gauze. She had just settled upon the gauze when her eye was taken by a bolt of mustard yellow grosgrain.

"Now, that," she exclaimed, "is all the go in London! All the fashionables are wearing it."

Miss Standish followed her gaze and repressed a shudder. "One can see why—I believe that they are quite willing to make guys of themselves in their attempts to set a fashion. Only a quiz could get themselves up in such a horrid color. It would spoil even such lovely coloring as yours, Clarissa. You are quite right to avoid it."

Clarissa abruptly discarded all notion of buying the offending material and decided upon the blush pink, while Madame Jeanne's black eyes twinkled approvingly. A little later, while ribbons and accessories were being chosen and Clarissa was deep in discussion with the dressmaker's young assistant, she murmured in Miss Standish's ear that there was also a little sage green day dress intended for the absent lady.

"We can do business, yes?" she suggested discreetly, and recognizing a bargain, Amy hastily agreed.

Some time later, their purchases about to be delivered to the Red Lion by the assistant, the ladies made their way back to the street stalls, intent upon honoring their promise to Penn. Mindful of her own recent childhood, Clarissa purchased a brightly painted spinning top, and Amy, who had intended to buy something instructive, like one of the new map jigsaw puzzles, gave way to impulse and bought a wooden musket, real enough to delight any boy's heart.

A small boy had supervised their purchases, offering friendly advice, and conscious of her unusually full purse, Amy was able for once to be generous and dropped a penny into his hand. The child thanked her with an engaging smile, reminding her, with his fair curls and delicate features, and despite the dirt that disfigured them, of the angels carved above monuments in churches.

"What a beautiful child!" she exclaimed as he ran to the next stall to buy a sugar-stick. "Is he yours?"

"No, miss—he lives across the way." The stall-holder indicated a butcher's shop opposite them. "An imp of Satan, he is, too! Shouldn't be out now, neither—his ma's already looked out twice. Hey, Jemmie," he called over his shoulder. "Yer ma's after you." The child bit off a lump from his candy-stick, thrust the rest into his pocket, and took to his heels. The man shook his head, saying, with a hint of admiration in his voice: "Looks like an angel, too, don't he?"

"Won't he get lost?" questioned Amy, watching the flying figure.

"Not him," answered the man. "Knows what's what, he does and never goes beyond the stalls."

Which was why, when they saw a tall man bend to speak to the boy and then suddenly scoop him up under one long arm, their interest was aroused. For a moment Amy wondered if it could be the child's father, but quickly realized that this ragged, grimy man could hardly claim kin to the respectably dressed boy, who by now was crying out in high-pitched shrieks of rage, his legs flailing uselessly as he was borne swiftly into the narrow entrance of an alleyway leading off the main street. Without pausing to think, she called out and ran after him. The man glanced over his shoulder and put on a spurt of speed.

"Get help!" Amy cried to Clarissa and hurried after the quickly vanishing figure.

The alley was narrow and twisting, overhung by the upper story of old buildings and thickly strewn with rubbish and oddments discarded by the families who lived there. Miss Standish was smaller and lighter than her quarry and not encumbered by a struggling, noisy burden. When she was near enough, she caught the flapping skirt of the long overcoat the man wore and gave it a hearty tug. Caught off balance, the man tumbled backward, sending his pursuer flying against the wall and losing his hold on the boy.

"Run, Jemmie!" commanded Miss Standish as the child scrambled to his feet, but instead of obeying her, the boy dashed back to his abductor and dealt him an enthusiastic kick on the ankle.

With a howl of pain, the man lunged forward and caught him by the collar before he could twist away. "Got ye, ye little varmit," he grunted with satisfaction. "And you, miss—keep yer distance," he warned, sparing Amy a glance as he pulled the struggling child toward him. Apparently thinking that the slight form of Miss Standish presented no danger, he turned his back on her and gave the boy, who had set up a shrill piping, a swift, hard cuff over the ear. "Shut yer trap," he snarled.

Realizing that action was needed, Amy took a silent step forward, and raising the toy musket, which by good fortune she had not discarded in her pursuit, she brought it down with all her strength on the stained crown of the man's wide-brimmed, disreputable hat. The thick felt absorbed most of the blow, but even so, the man staggered a few steps before turning a look of astonishment upon his attacker.

The stories she had heard from her soldier father of successful charges rose clearly in Amy's heated mind, and, baring her teeth, she raised her weapon aloft in an unsoldierly fashion and, with a wild cry,

55

ran at the man. A gratifying look of alarm spread over his face, and throwing his captive from him, he took to his heels and fled. Amy was dimly aware of a masculine shout and someone crashing past her, as Jemmie hurtled into her arms, and realized, with chagrin, that she had not been the cause of the abductor's ignominious retreat.

A shaken Clarissa arrived and clutched at her shoulder, almost incoherent with fright. "Oh, Aunt Almeria, are you alright?" she gasped. "Oh—what a thing to happen. *Just* like a novel ... I w-was never more f-frightened in my life!"

At that moment the man who had rushed past Amy, putting her victim to flight, returned and she saw that he was a slim, young man in a naval uniform of blue jacket and white breeches, one arm supported in a black silk sling. Although panting and slightly disheveled, he made a creditable bow and began to introduce himself just as Jemmie's mother arrived in the alley, accompanied by a shouting, gesticulating crowd and, at that moment, Clarissa chose to close her eyes and grow alarmingly pale.

With commendable promptness, the lieutenant leaped forward and caught her swaying form in his free arm. Amy could not but admire how beautifully the dark blue of his uniform set off Clarissa's blond coloring and pink bonnet as he supported her against his chest. Releasing Jemmie into his mother's care, she searched in her reticule for her vinaigrette and, unstopping the tiny bottle, held it under Clarissa's nose.

Above the drooping head, gray eyes met hers. "Well done," he said with approval. "The child
56

would have been stolen but for your quick action, Miss—?" he finished on a note of inquiry.

"Standish. Am—Almeria Standish," Amy supplied, watching as color returned to her charge's cheeks and blue eyes opened to gaze blankly up at the anxious face above her.

"Where—?" she began before, recovering quickly, she flushed and made an effort to free herself.

Having heard the tale of his adventures from her offspring, Mrs. Peel descended upon Amy, enveloping her in a huge hug, all the while thanking her tearfully.

"The lieutenant here was instrumental in setting the villain to flight," Amy told her, replacing her bonnet, which Mrs. Peel's enthusiasm had knocked crooked. "Now, Jemmie, promise me to do as your mother tells you in the future," she admonished the adventurer, who showed his good sense by dissolving into wild sobs, which distracted his fond mother from all thoughts of punishment.

"Allow me the honor of escorting you home," begged the lieutenant, gazing at Clarissa with solicitude.

"Our carriage is at the Red Lion," Amy informed him and felt called upon to introduce Clarissa, who still clung nervously to his arm. "I must make my charge known to you," she began, as they walked along the high street.

"I have some slight acquaintance with Miss Clarissa—and indeed with Sir Hugo Dysart, as I have recently rented Peninsula House and so can count myself a neighbor."

Clarissa looked up. "Penn's house!" she exclaimed. "I knew that Hugo intended to let it." Recovering her animation, she sent her escort a sparkling glance. "How delightful it will be to have one of our sailor heroes as a tenant. Pray do call upon us—seamen always have such exciting stories to tell and country society is so dull."

"I shall look forward to calling at Candover Magna," the lieutenant told them and, by dint of skillful maneuvering, extricated them from the crowd that had followed them in order to hear Mrs. Peel's repeated thanks. The short walk back to the Red Lion was managed comfortably under his guidance, Clarissa's shaken nerves steadied by his calm manner and diverting conversation.

Miss Standish, who had been ready to intervene should he prove to be too forward in his approach, was relieved to find that he treated her charge with the gentlemanly regard due to her age and position, showing no disposition to flirt or take advantage of her youthful high spirits, which had returned now that the adventure was over and she could happily recall every exciting moment.

By the time they arrived at the inn, they were fast becoming firm friends, and Clarissa had quite recovered and could thank him prettily for his company. Touching a hand to his cocked hat in a salute that went straight to the ladies' hearts, he left them and shortly Tedbury brought the chaise to the door.

"What a *very* nice-mannered man, to be sure," remarked Clarissa, settling back in her seat. "And really quite handsome. How do you suppose he came by the hurt to his arm?"

"Some act of daring, I am sure," responded Amy obligingly.

"I have never been acquainted with a naval man before. His air of quiet consequence is quite refreshing after the—*brashness* of the redcoats one is always meeting in Town." She paused before adding, a little doubtfully: "Though to be honest, I do find his name somewhat unusual."

"Really? What was it? There was so much noise when he spoke it, besides that fact that you chose that moment to feel faint, that I did not pay attention."

"Shovell," supplied Clarissa, eyeing her repressively.

"Oh—well, to be sure, that is a *little unusual*, but I believe that there was a Sir Cloudsly Shovell, who was in command of a ship that sank off the Scilly Isles a hundred years or so ago," Miss Standish said with commendable gravity. "Though being a sailor himself, he may not care to recall the incident. I mentioned it merely to show that the name, while odd, may be illustrious too!" she finished fair-mindedly.

This seemed to please Clarissa, who brightened perceptibly and remarked that she had supposed that Lieutenant Shovell had come from an aristocratic family all along. "Were not his manners charming? And how easily he managed things for us. What good fortune that I happened upon him when you dashed off like that. I must own that I was quite startled when you ran off down that dark alleyway and if he had not come to my aid, asking if he could be of assistance, I really do not know what I would have done—for it was the first time that I had ever found myself alone, you know."

Reflecting that her charge obviously could not be relied upon in an emergency, Amy allowed her thoughts to wander, thinking happily of her purchases, which would be delivered as soon as the slight alterations had been made. She was recalled to her surroundings by the carriage swinging round a corner and realized that they were almost home.

Clarissa, who was eager to recount the tale of her adventure, which had grown in excitement during their journey, leaped down from the chaise and ran indoors, followed more sedately by Miss Standish, who found her charge morosely surveying a mound of luggage in the hall.

"Lucius!" Clarissa declared gloomily. "What can have brought him here?"

CHAPTER FOUR

"I brought Miss Witherspoon. I thought you would have need of her," Lucius replied virtuously to the same question a few hours later, when Clarissa happened to meet him in the hall on her way into dinner. "And you need not look at me like that, Clarissa, for the woman insisted that I bring your luggage, too."

"Withy—but where is she?" cried the girl, looking round as if expecting to find her governess lurking in the shadows that filled the far corners.

"How should I know?" was the testy reply. "Maybe Hugo has given her notice, which is only what she deserves. They have been closeted together since we arrived, with that secretary fellow in attendance."

The door to the study opened as he spoke and Sir Hugo and a slighter, soberly dressed man appeared. Amy noticed that they were both in evening dress and concluded that, like herself, the secretary was expected to dine with the family. The men seemed on the best of terms with each other, and before he came forward to give his hand to his sister, Sir Hugo clapped the other on the shoulder, advising him to make all haste about some unspecified business.

"Well, Clary," he began, holding out his hand. "Have you spent all your allowance?"

"Hugo, what is this about poor Withy?" she began ominously, ignoring his proffered aid as she descended the last few steps of the staircase. "Even you could not be such a blackguard as to make her suffer for my misdemeanor!"

"I had not thought it suffering, precisely," he returned mildly.

His sister regarded him with withering contempt. "To cast the poor woman off! When you *know* that she never could keep me under control, even when I was in short skirts! If anyone is to blame, it is *you*, for setting us all in a tangle."

Sir Hugo frowned, but before he could reply a door was closed upstairs and feet could be heard hurrying along the corridor. A tall, angular figure appeared at the head of the stairs and began to descend, talking all the while.

"Oh, Clarissa, my dear, I was never more glad to see anyone. . . . Not that I would wish anyone to think that I am *not* pleased to see Sir Hugo and Mr. Gambrill—and dear Mr. Fifield and—and Miss Standish, have I got it right? How do you do, Miss Standish, we have not met, but I am very pleased to know you." Pausing to untangle a long, floating scarf from the newel post, she surveyed the people below, an unbecoming blush suffusing her face at finding herself the object of the concerted gaze. "Oh, dear—am I late? I would not keep you waiting, for the world—" She dropped her reticule, which tumbled down the stairs, coming to rest at Sir Hugo's feet.

"Come down, Miss Witherspoon," he said, bending to retrieve her property. "You have not kept us waiting." He held his hand out as she still hesitated and smiled encouragement. "You will make our cousin think me an ogre," he chided, returning her reticule to her as she finally reached the last step. "Cousin Almeria, let me introduce Miss Witherspoon, who has been Clarissa's governess for many years."

As she bowed and exchanged smiles with the older woman, Amy could not help wondering at Sir Hugo's unexpected forbearance in the face of such intense nervousness.

"Do not worry, Withy," put in Clarissa, coming forward to take her arm. "All will be well, I promise you."

"How kind—but then, you always were the sweetest child, so sorry almost as soon as you had lost your temper. Such news, Clarissa ... when I traveled here in trepidation, fearful that—well, I should *not* have mentioned certain things to you, I realize that, but at the time it seemed so romantic. But now, to receive such kindness has quite shaken me and I do not know how to thank Sir Hugo enough."

"For what?" demanded Clarissa of her brother.

"Let Miss Witherspoon tell you over tea," he suggested, dismissing the subject. "We have kept dinner waiting long enough and I, for one, do not care for cold meat."

Amy found herself seated next to Sir Hugo's secretary, a sober, self-possessed man, a little older than his employer. Lucius was next to Clarissa and set out to amuse her, with little success as she paid him scant attention, being preoccupied with sending her brother suspicious glances.

At last Sir Hugo looked up and encountered her

frowning gaze. "Do not glower at me, Clary," he said. "If you are seeking to intimidate me with that thunderous expression, let me tell you it will not work—"

"I will not let you do it," she cried and he raised his eyebrows at such unexpected passion.

"Of course, I always do as my little sister commands," he replied blandly. "How useful it would be if I knew to what you were referring."

"Withy—Miss Witherspoon—you intend to dismiss her and—and I will *not* allow it!"

He regarded her with blatant weariness. "What a foolish child you are. If it were not for your obvious care for another person, I would send you to your room until you remember your manners!" he remarked in a drawl that made her eyes flash. "You would do well to be sure of your facts before attacking me, my dear Clarissa."

"Do you deny that you have turned off Miss Witherspoon?" she demanded hotly.

"Dearest Clarissa, *pray* do not ..." Mary Witherspoon fluttered and dropped her fork in her agitation.

"Miss Witherspoon and I have come to an amicable agreement," Sir Hugo told his sister in withering tones, "with which I understand she is quite happy."

"More—more than happy, dear Sir Hugo," interposed the older woman. "So kind—such condescension ... More than I ever ..."

"And now the matter is closed," said his lordship. "If Miss Witherspoon chooses to make it known to you, doubtless she will." Having sent Clarissa an intimidating look, he turned to his secretary and asked in a lighter voice what news he brought from London.

"The newspapers are full of the war, of course. Napoleon is on the run and the general feeling is that it cannot last much longer. Now that Wellington has bypassed Bayonne, there can be no stopping him taking Paris."

Sir Hugo gave a harsh bark of laughter. "I hear that they are trying Congreve's rockets again—they should certainly frighten the horses, if only they can be persuaded to fly in the right direction!"

"What of the navy?" Clarissa startled them by asking suddenly. "Have there been any sea battles recently?"

"I believe that the naval blockades go on," returned James Fifield with his usual courtesy.

"Why the interest?" asked Sir Hugo. "I've never known you to care about anything other than the next dance or the color of a dress." He scrutinized her closely. "Do you number a sailor among your beaus?" he speculated.

Clarissa was only too ready to recount the tale of their adventure and meeting with Lieutenant Shovell, who had assumed the mantle of a knight-errant in the meantime.

"Shovell? I do not recall a *Shovell*," said her brother, searching his mind.

"You must," his sister told him impatiently, "for he says you have let him Penn's house." Sir Hugo's expression changed but Clarissa did not notice and, intent upon her desire that the lieutenant should be accepted at Candover Magna, hurried on: "As a neighbor he would be welcome here, would he not? Especially having performed a singular service to me—to us. Aunt Almeria thought him a gentleman of the first water. Did you not?" She appealed to Amy for confirmation.

65

"Well, Cousin, we are waiting for your opinion," put in Sir Hugo as Amy hesitated. "Did you think this . . . *Shovell* a suitable person to be acquainted with my sister?"

Something in his voice made her study his face and she was almost certain that behind the carefully blank expression, he was amused. "Those would not be my words, but he seemed a very pleasant young man," she returned noncommittally. "His manners were exceptional and he made no attempt to encroach upon the acquaintance thrust upon him by the circumstances."

Clarissa waited with bated breath, searching her brother's face as he considered.

"As you say, I *am* acquainted with Mr. . . . er, Shovell," he began judiciously. Turning to his secretary he asked: "What was your opinion, James?"

"Of whom, sir?" Mr. Fifield appeared puzzled.

"The gentleman who has rented Peninsula House," replied his employer evenly.

Again a note in his voice caught Miss Standish's attention and she noticed a meaningful glance quickly exchanged between the two men.

"A very pleasant young man, I thought," James Fifield supplied after the briefest of pauses.

"And one of our heroes, I thought you said," murmured Sir Hugo. "Wounded in some naval encounter, no doubt?"

"No doubt," returned the secretary gravely, but Amy was almost certain that his mouth twitched slightly and could not but help wondering what amusement could be passing between them.

"Does it matter?" demanded Mr. Gambrill in fretful tones. "What can the fellow's antecedents have to do with us? Surely, Hugo, you intend to remove back to Town, and Clarissa can hardly entertain without your presence."

"Ah, now there, my dear Lucius, you are mistaken in assuming that I will return to London. You could not know, but I have lately spent much time here. Indeed, I find country living quite to my liking. There are always diversions to be had on the estate, I find."

Clarissa sat up. "Really, Hugo?" she cried. "Then we could hold a dance—oh, *do* say so! It would be above all things splendid!" Clasping her hands, she looked at her brother hopefully, all her previous annoyance with him forgotten.

Hugo smiled at her. "You are leaving yourself wide open to blackmail," he pointed out lazily. "Clarissa, my dear, if you are good, do exactly as I bid, act me no Cheltenham tragedies, and do not cause me irritation in any way . . . I may consider some kind of entertainment."

"Fudge! I am not taken in by such nonsense!" she told him roundly. "You would not tease, dearest brother, if you were not prepared to countenance it! What a good thing that I ordered a new evening gown only this morning!"

The meal progressed in a lightened atmosphere, various ideas being put forward as to the precise nature of the proposed entertainment. Clarissa would not be turned from the glories of a supperdance, Lucius proposed a formal dinner for the cream of local society, Mr. Fifield voted for a musical evening with a professional singer and quartet as the main attraction, and Miss Witherspoon, quite forgetting her diffidence, proclaimed the joys of a masquerade ball.

Amy, who had just recalled that while in Winchester she had forgotten to post the letter she had written to her mother, and that the news of her own whereabouts and a description of Penn was still reposing in her reticule, became aware that all attention was on her. The room was silent, while the occupants obviously waited for her to speak.

Seeing her confusion, Sir Hugo repeated his question. "We were waiting for your suggestion, Cousin," he said, adding helpfully as she looked about rather wildly for inspiration: "About the nature of the evening party."

"A—a skating party," she replied quickly, without consideration.

There was silence round the table, then it was pointed out that snow and ice would be needed for such a proposition.

"Of course, but I believe that the consensus among the country folk I heard talking today was that the cold weather was sure to return," she said, defending her spur-of-the-moment idea.

"It would certainly be very unusual," put in Mr. Fifield, taking gentlemanly pity on her, and Clarissa, who had been turning the matter over in her head, nodded enthusiastically.

"Even if the river did not freeze over, there is an old sleigh in the coach-house and I am almost sure it was trying to snow on the way home this afternoon. . . . No one has ever held a—a Winter Party before."

"No, indeed," agreed her brother. "You would doubtless become famous overnight for having thought of such a thing! How enchanting—if only the weather would be so kind as to oblige!"

"A Winter Masquerade would be just the thing,"

observed Miss Witherspoon, giving way to a flight of fancy. "Everyone could wear white or silver."

"My new dress is pink," objected Clarissa, "though to be sure, it would be the prettiest thing."

"I have not yet agreed," put in his lordship, ending speculation and holding up his hand as Clarissa was about to burst into impassioned speech. "No more, Sister. I will consider an evening entertainment of some kind, but only if the matter is now dropped and you do not plague me."

Although she burned to have the matter settled, she was wise enough to say no more on the subject, instead recounting the tale of Penn's delight upon being presented with his new spinning top and slightly battered toy musket.

The story brought speculation about the motive behind the attempted abduction, which Sir Hugo brought to an end by stating that the child had obviously been wanted for use as a pitiful beggar.

"You both remarked upon his beauty," he pointed out. "It is obvious that such a child would tug at the hearts of susceptible people. I have heard of it happening in London or other big cities; I am only surprised that it should take place in so respectable a town as Winchester."

His gaze seemed to dwell on Amy as he spoke, and she had the uneasy suspicion that he intended to question her further about their adventure. However, she had first to listen to Miss Witherspoon's tale, that lady bursting into speech as soon as they left the gentlemen to their port.

"Only think," she began as they crossed the hall. "Such kindness is more than could be expected. . . . How can I ever thank dear Sir Hugo for his magnanimity? That I should open a little school has long been my ambition, but I little thought . . . for it to happen! How noble, how kind!"

She was still expressing her gratification when the men rejoined the ladies as the tea tray was brought in, and Sir Hugo took the opportunity to bring Miss Standish a cup of tea and draw her a little apart from the general group.

"Recount to me your version of the tale," he commanded, leading her to a sofa slightly distant from the other occupants of the room, who had grouped themselves around the fireplace. "I imagine it is somewhat different to Clarissa's account."

Seeing that there was nothing else to be done, Amy told him the bald details, only omitting the circumstance of how the wooden musket came to be damaged.

His eyes narrowed at her reticence. "And the musket, Cousin, how did that sustain the chip in its paint-work?"

Amy eyed him warily. "It came into contact with the wall of the alley," she told him truthfully.

His mouth twitched. "It is more than fortunate that it did not come into contact with the fellow's skull!" he remarked, confirming her suspicion that he had an astute idea as to the cause.

"It would not have been more than the wretch deserved," she said. "To do such a thing—to attempt to carry off a child so blatantly, in full daylight, speaks of a wickedness that is beyond contemplation. If we had not been there, I dread to think what might have happened to Jemmie, who you must know is a game little boy—why, instead of running off when I told him to, he picked himself up and returned to deliver a kick to his abductor's ankles!"

70

"Very resourceful," commented Sir Hugo dryly. "And while this was happening, I take it that Clarissa was indulging in hysterics somewhere."

"No such thing—I am afraid that I left her in the high street, which you may not think I should have done, but I am sure she would have come to no harm and it was there that she found Mr. Shovell and, with the greatest presence of mind, sent him to my aid." Amy looked up at Sir Hugo thoughtfully. "Why do you find that so amusing?" she could not help asking.

A disarming grin appeared, but her employer shook his head. "My sister shows all the familiar signs of having been heart-smitten. I own to looking forward to seeing her renew her acquaintance with this paragon of her own devising, who threatens to unseat Kit Masters. . . . It will be interesting to see if the naval hero retains his romantic aura upon closer knowledge. Clarissa is a romantic little fool, Cousin . . . as I think you are well aware."

"You are too harsh, sir."

"Nonsense, Cousin Almeria."

She looked up quickly at the bantering tone in his voice and, meeting his mocking gaze, felt the heat rise in her cheeks.

"Do you object to me calling you cousin?" he asked. "If you are to act out the part, you must accept the familiar title."

"Why did the wretched girl saddle me with such a name? Jane or Mary or even Fanny would have served the purpose."

"Ah, but she obviously felt none of those suited you. Almeria has a particular ring to it—its owner must be elegant, attractive—and mysterious!"

Amy blinked and wondered for one wild moment

71

if he was flirting with her, before realizing that he could only be amusing himself. Not until later was she to remember and wonder at that final "mysterious." Lifting her chin indignantly, she stared coldly at Sir Hugo. "Remember, sir, that I did not choose it. However unsuitable you may consider it, it was chosen for me."

Not used to being given a set-down, Sir Hugo snapped his black eyebrows together in a frown and his gray eyes darkened. "By the by," he began, his voice as frosty as his expression. "Mr. Fifield tells me that it has been difficult to take up your references."

Suitably put in her place, Amy could only look at him. "Neither can that be put at my door," she said steadily, safe in the knowledge that her references were genuine.

"It is a little odd, you will allow. All your previous employers seem to have either moved or left the country."

"I daresay that they had not considered that their erstwhile governess would have need of a forwarding address," she returned. "I know that Mrs. Melville was desirous of joining her husband who is attached to the General's staff—Lady Witchett may have returned to her native Scotland—as for the others . . . I have no idea."

"You appear to have stayed in no position for long," he remarked.

"Girls about to come out have little need of a long-term companion," she pointed out reasonably, but her heart began to flutter at the prospect of losing contact with Penn after having regained it only so recently.

Sir Hugo would have said more, but Clarissa

called to him to settle an argument and he joined his sister beside the fire. To Amy, he was a looming presence for the rest of the evening. Several times she was aware of being the object of his bleak gaze and was relieved when the party broke up. Following Clarissa up the stairs, she mentioned the letter she had forgotten to post in Winchester that morning and was advised to leave it on the hall table and Sir Hugo would frank it before one of the grooms took the bag of mail to the post office the next morning.

The letter continued to bother her, and having first decided to wait until morning to take it to the hall, she altered her mind, thinking that the groom might set off before she was awake. Thankful that she had not undressed, she took up her candle and, with the letter in her hands, ran down the stairs. The fire had burned low, only a faint glimmer of red showed among the ashes, and the flickering light from her candle only served to accentuate the height and breadth of the huge hall, making no inroads on the thick, black shadows that seemed to close round her.

Miss Standish was not given to nerves, but having paused on the last tread of the stairs, she had to admit to a reluctance to step down into the velvet black void. An uneasy cold prickle made itself felt between her shoulder blades, filling her with the certainty that she was being watched and, turning her head abruptly, she saw a figure leaning over the banister above her. She had a confused impression of an indeterminate form that was lighter than its dark surroundings, of something long and slender shining, and then a murmur of voices arose as the door of the study opened, light cut across the

73

darkness as Sir Hugo and his secretary walked into the hall.

"Good God, Cousin, what are you doing there?" exclaimed the taller man. "You look as if you have seen a ghost!"

"I—I think I may have," Amy returned, her voice shaking slightly. "D-do you have a resident one, complete with shining sword?"

There was a pause. "As it happens, we do," began James Fifield, but Sir Hugo cut across him.

"I see someone has made known the tale," he said coldly. "It will do you no good, let me tell you, ma'am. I am no believer in superstition."

It was not until the next morning that Amy found out to what he was alluding; Clarissa appeared as she was pinning up her hair and, after watching her critically for a while, remarked that a softer style would suit her better.

"I daresay, but I am a paid companion, not a lady of fashion," Amy told her and, reaching for the last pin, exclaimed as she noticed the letter reposing again on her dressing table. "Wretched thing—I believe that you have a determination not to be posted!" she cried and recounted her nighttime adventure.

Clarissa's blue eyes opened wide as the story progressed, and despite her companion's attempt to make light of the affair, she nodded solemnly. "It was Sir Hugo—" she began thrillingly.

"No, it was not," Amy told her impatiently. "Sir Hugo and Mr. Fifield came out of the study."

"No, no—not *Hugo*. Sir Hugo, who was a Cavalier and fought for the king. He was killed at Edgehill and appeared here to his betrothed to tell her to marry his brother. Since then he has appeared to the Dysart brides." She gave Amy a thoughtful look.

Amy gave a short laugh. "I can see why Sir Hugo disclaimed all belief in such things!" she admitted ruefully.

But when the ladies went down for breakfast, he seemed to have forgotten the incident, instead asking if Clarissa had happened to look out of the window that morning.

Going across the morning room and drawing back the curtain, she exclaimed with joy. "It's snowing!" she cried, clapping her hands and turning back to the table, her face alight. "I shall have a Snow Party after all!"

"Don't count your chickens too soon, sister mine," her brother advised. "It will take at least three days of deep cold to make the river safe for skating."

All that day Clarissa could hardly sit still, continuously gazing out of the nearest window at the flurries of snow beating against the glass and wondering aloud as to the length the cold spell would last.

By next morning there appeared no doubt that the party could go ahead, Tedbury having taken it upon himself to inspect the river and reporting that the ice was nearly strong enough to bear his weight. However, a new problem arose; the snow refused to stop. Soon Clarissa was in despair that anyone would be able to travel the snowbound roads and Miss Standish, who had regretted her suggestion almost as soon as it had been made, began to wish heartily that she had not been surprised into making the proposal.

At last the heavy clouds rolled away, blue sky

appeared, and the sun shone on the cold, white world. Sir Hugo put in an appearance and demanded the list of guests over which Clarissa had spent agonizing hours.

"You have included the Masters, I see," he commented quietly, running his eyes over the paper.

"Oh, Hugo!" his sister wailed. "How could I not? I don't even know if Kit is there. *Please* let me invite them."

He smiled down into her anxious face. "You may invite the Masters, provided you ask Lieutenant Shovell as well," he said.

"*Dearest* of brothers," she retorted, "cast your eyes down a little. He is already there! Do you really think that I would leave such a catch as a newcomer in the form of a personable young man off my list? You must know that he will be the main attraction, for as far as I know, no one else has had the felicity of meeting him."

Her brother laughed. "Your fame as a hostess is made!" he teased and tossed the list into her lap.

As soon as he had left the room, she set about the pleasant task of writing the invitations. Miss Witherspoon having shown herself willing to help, Amy felt able to suggest that Penn might like a turn around the snow-covered garden, proposing to take him herself.

Clarissa looked doubtful. "Miss James is very careful of him," she said. "I doubt that she would approve."

"I'll ask Sir Hugo," replied Amy, thinking that if she was armed with Penn's guardian's approval, the governess could not very well raise objections. Brought up to believe in the benefits of fresh air

76

and exercise, she suspected that both would do Penn some good.

Sir Hugo seemed surprised by her request, and looking at her steadily, half turned in his chair from the papers on his desk.

"The sun is shining and if he is wrapped warmly, I am sure he will take no harm," she said in defense of her proposal, taking his silence for disagreement.

"I do not disapprove," he told her. "I was wondering why you should make the offer."

Amy looked down at her clasped hands. "You consider it not my place—I am sorry if you think it interfering of me. Of course Miss James must have control of his activities . . . but I am, as far as she is aware, his relation." She turned to go, but her employer's voice stopped her before she could turn the doorknob.

"Wait!" Sir Hugo said imperiously. "Do you have much experience of small boys?"

"I have two younger brothers," she replied, a little surprised by the abrupt question.

"Then, tell me—what do you think of Penn's health?"

"I—can hardly say. I do not know him. I have heard Miss James state that he is delicate." She could not keep the note of doubt from her voice.

"As a mere male, and one with little experience of young children, it seems to me that the boy is being turned into an invalid! I fear his governess mollycoddles him!"

Amy Standish agreed, but felt that caution was called for. "I do feel that with care, fresh air is beneficial for everyone," she said carefully.

"Precisely. Penn should not spend all his time
77

shut up in the nursery. Take the boy out with my blessing, Cousin."

Amy found Penn listlessly practicing pothooks on a sheet of paper. His expression brightened when he saw her and when he understood her errand, he jumped to his feet with a whoop of excitement. Miss James was far from pleased, her mouth tightening at this unwelcome interruption.

"Penn's chest is weak," she protested. "The cold will give him a chill."

"I promise to take care to wrap him up warmly."

"I will not be responsible for any harm that may come to him."

"To be sure not," Amy agreed, buttoning her nephew into his overcoat and wrapping an oversize red scarf across his chest and tying the ends around his waist as she had often done for her brothers. Gloves and a peaked cap with a tassle completed his outfit and she smiled down into his eager face. "You look just like a round robin redbreast," she told him and, taking his hand, led him to her own room where she attired herself in her warmest coat and stepped into a pair of high, wooden pattens, worn over her shoes to lift her out of the snow.

The paths near the house had been swept and so Amy and Penn could walk freely between high banks of snow and tall evergreen hedges. The sun was warm on their faces and struck bright sparks on the white covering that decorated walls and trees as if a confectioner had run mad with sugar icing. Penn was delighted to be free of the confines of the house, and kicking at the snow with his sturdy boots, he sent it flying with crows of joy. Mindful of her promise, Amy soon turned back to-

78

ward the house, pleased that, beyond one protest, the child was willing to obey.

Taking her hand, he skipped alongside her, his nose above the red scarf pink with the cold air. "I like the snow," he confided. "Can we come out again? Looking out of the window does *not* please me."

"If you are a good boy and work hard for Miss James, we shall take another walk tomorrow."

"I expect I will take cold," he reported gloomily. "I always *do*."

"Oh, surely not!" exclaimed his companion, shocked by his expectation.

"And have to take to my bed and eat only bread and milk—*yuk!*"

Miss Standish studied his woebegone expression and bent to hug him against her side. "Not this time," she assured him. "You cannot have taken cold in ten minutes. I promise no bed—and no bread and milk!"

Penn seemed unconvinced; mounting the stairs with gathering despondency, he announced at the top of his voice as soon as he entered the nursery that Aunt Almy said he had not taken cold.

Somewhat embarrassed, Amy confirmed that he was as "warm as toast" and unwrapped him. "Only feel his hands, Miss James."

The governess sniffed. "Doubtless we will see to-morrow," she announced, not mollified by Amy's gesture. "I only hope that he is not feverish in the night."

"No chance of that," replied Amy, determinedly cheerful, "such good care you have taken of him!" and she reminded Penn of her promise to repeat the excursion on the morrow.

CHAPTER FIVE

Amy had expected that the thick snow would present difficulties and prevent people from traveling to the party, but she found that the country folk were used to winter conditions and most families had provided themselves with a sledge, or particularly heavy coach for just such weather. The invitations were eagerly accepted, the reply from Mrs. Masters bringing Clarissa especial joy when she read that Kit would be among her guests; she only needed an acceptance from Peninsula House to complete her happiness.

Watching the weather anxiously, the ladies of the household flung themselves into preparations for the party. Mrs. Hill was consulted and told what fare to provide; the head gardener, a somewhat curmudgeonly man, was persuaded to take on the task of setting up a bonfire to provide light and warmth for the skaters as well as a means of cooking a side of beef; the grooms polished and repaired an ancient sledge, which was to be used to give rides on the river. Tables and chairs were set up in the garden pavilion, which, as Clarissa pointed out, by great good fortune overlooked the river. Sir Hugo, Lucius, and Mr. Fifield became very preoccupied with manly tasks that took them out of the house for most of the day, until at last Clarissa despaired of their searching out the family skates, which had long reposed in the attics.

"It's too bad!" she exclaimed, having found that they had escaped yet again. "I am determined to wait no longer or we shall be the only ones without skates and how would that look? I shall search them out myself." Her determined walk faltered as she hesitated in the doorway. "Only ... I've never cared for the attics, such great, gloomy caverns as they are, with ancient furniture and moldy trunks to remind one of every Gothic story ever read! So, *pray*, dear Aunt Almeria, keep me company."

Always having had a liking, not often indulged, for such places, Amy was perfectly willing to accompany her charge and found, rather to her surprise, that Clarissa's description had not been exaggerated. The attics of Candover Magna were indeed cavernous, with huge arched beams reminding her of a church. Light, dimly filtering through small windows at either end, failed to illuminate the dark interior, for every corner was filled with thick, black shadows and the ladies were glad that they had had the forethought to provide themselves with candles.

Once the candles were lit, and despite her professed fears, Clarissa bustled about until she found the skates, and then her attention was taken by the sight of her old toys lying in a corner and she exclaimed happily over her various finds.

"I declare here is dear old Neddy—what a pity Penn has a new rocking horse. I vow it is nowhere near as delightful as this fellow! What rides I had! And only look in this box—filled with my dolls." After rummaging in the box, she produced a battered manikin, arrayed in the remains of a fashionable gown. "Arabella Melancholy—I remember how exquisitely elegant I thought her name—had a whole wardrobe of clothes."

Forgetting the task that had brought them to the top of the house, she dropped the skates and sat on the floor to dress the sharp-nosed doll in her worn finery of yellow, hooped petticoat and cream brocade overdress, such as Clarissa's grandmother might have worn. After a moment Amy wandered away, running her fingers over the dusty tops of outmoded tables, examining piles of discarded curtains, obviously thought at one time too good to be thrown away, but now thick with grime and smelling of must, and came upon a large picture frame leaning against the wall. As she pulled off the cloth that covered it, she could not suppress an exclamation of astonishment as she found herself looking at Sir Hugo's features, gazing at her with that expression of arrogant amusement with which she was fast becoming familiar.

"How can this be?" she asked, puzzled. "Was it taken from fancy dress?"

Clarissa looked over her shoulder. "That is the Cavalier," she said, examining it critically. "I had not realized how Hugo resembles him, but you are right. Without those ridiculous lovelocks and all that lace and ribbon, they are as like as two peas!"

"Why is it here?" asked Amy. "I would have thought it would be kept in the hall with the other family portraits."

"I believe it was brought up here after my mama encountered him one night before she married Papa—I daresay she thought it might discourage him from visiting the rest of the house!"

Amy looked at her curiously. "He does not worry you?"

Clarissa shrugged and spitting on her handkerchief, scrubbed at Arabella's wooden face. "Why should he?" she said simply. "He only appears to brides or future wives—never to family."

Hugo appeared somewhat indifferent to the story, but Lucius volunteered to go and get the portrait so that they all could judge its likeness for themselves. He was gone some time and when he finally reappeared and presented the oil painting with a flourish, it was gazed at silently. Sir Hugo raised an eyebrow and leaning his chin on his hand, surveyed his ancestor with wry amusement.

"What a dandy," he remarked. "It always amazes me that they were able to move in those furbelows, let alone fight—and by all accounts, he was one of the heroes of Edgehill."

"Such a likeness," proclaimed Miss Witherspoon thrillingly. "So romantic and handsome, even if the costume is a little—not, of course, that I mean . . . The very last thing I would ever do is to question his—Oh, dear!" Realizing where her tongue was leading her, she blushed and started again, doing her best to redeem herself. "Without the clothes, which, we must agree, are the slightest bit feminine, which, of course, was all the fashion—I am sure he would be reckoned the most masculine of men . . . and so like our own dear Sir Hugo!"

"Very astute of you, ma'am," put in Sir Hugo. "How right you are—I believe that his wedding was a very sudden affair, not altogether to be explained by the war, and that his son was one of those seven-month babies that abound in even the best of families!"

83

While she retired behind her wineglass to hide her blushes, Clarissa, who had been studying the portrait, made a discovery. "I do believe that he is wearing your ring, Hugo."

"Of course. All the heads of the family wear it." He extended one hand and displayed the heavy gold ring, set with a large cabochon ruby. "I think we'll put him back in his proper place in the hall."

"I only hope it may not set him to walking again," said Miss Witherspoon with a shudder.

"According to the legend, you need have no fear of seeing him," put in Lucius unkindly.

"I am sure he will be so grateful to be out of the attic, which must be deadly boring, even if you are only a painting, that he will be on his best behavior," Clarissa assured her, with a glare at her cousin.

"I take it that you found the skates," said Sir Hugo, deftly turning the conversation.

His sister nodded. "I gave them to Hill to have cleaned and burnished."

"I remember that there is a pair to fit a small child—I would prefer it if Penn did not see them. Julian nearly lost his life one winter, venturing onto the ice without supervision."

"If you would allow me, I would enjoy teaching him," Amy was surprised to hear herself say.

"The child has certainly won your heart," observed Lucius. "Miss James will feel usurped."

Amy became aware that her employer was studying her, his gray gaze intent. "It would be wise for us all to practice before committing ourselves to hosting an ice party. I, for one, intend to try the ice in the morning. Accompany me, Cousin, and bring

Penn, if you please. A guardian must have an especial care for his ward, as you must be aware."

A brief smile softened the words, but Amy recognized that she was not altogether trusted to be in sole charge of the small boy when there was a hint of possible danger and, wondering a little at the cause, determined to demonstrate to Sir Hugo her ability to look after his ward.

The next morning her nephew, once he realized the treat in store for him, was delirious with excitement, hopping from one foot to the other as she dressed him in his warm coat, barely able to control his eagerness to be off.

Miss James looked on with disapproval. "I do not agree with interrupting his schooling. He is not strong; no good can come of this constant activity."

Amy looked up as she knelt in front of Penn, tying his scarf. "I promise to take the greatest care—and you really need have no fear as to his safety, for Sir Hugo is to accompany us."

Knowing herself bested, Honora James sniffed and fell silent, her face set in lines of ill-concealed annoyance. "You must do an extra hour of arithmetic this afternoon, young man, to make up," she informed her pupil.

Not even the thought of extra lessons could dampen Penn's spirits as the schoolroom was left behind, and, collecting their skates, they let themselves out of the house by a side door and headed across the snow-covered park toward the river. As they approached, they saw a single figure gliding effortlessly over the ice and Penn caught his breath.

"Uncle Hugo!" he shrieked, dropping Amy's hand,

and she was only just in time to catch him and prevent his plunging onto the ice.

"Now, wait!" she cried firmly. "You must never run onto the ice without looking first. I am sure you know that water is dangerous; well, ice is even more so, for it looks quite hard and safe and yet can be so thin that even a little 'un like you would break it and fall through. You must *always* test it first and *never* go on it alone."

Sir Hugo had come up in time to hear her last words and nodded his approval. "Just so. Take heed of your wise aunt, Penn."

Heedless of the snow, Penn sat down and tried to strap his skates to his boots. With a laugh at his impatience, his uncle picked him up and, skating the few yards to a log that had been placed to serve as a convenient seat, performed the task for him.

By the time Amy had fastened on her own skates, they were in the center of the ice, the shouting, wobbly child being persuaded to take his first gliding steps by the tall man. Joining them, she took his other hand and, holding him between them, she and Sir Hugo set off along the frozen river.

Wind had blown the surface clear of snow and their skate blades sang crisply with each step. Overhead the sky was a clear eggshell blue, while the sparkling snow transformed the countryside into a magical land. Icicles hung from the trees and tinkled as they hit against each other when the breeze shook the branches. A robin perched on a twig, a bright ball of red and brown, before he darted off. A crow watched from the topmost branch of a bare tree, commenting loudly before he, too, flew away, his abrupt departure causing snow to fall from branch to branch until a small avalanche descended upon the skaters, and with a raucous laugh, the crow returned to his perch.

"One could almost think it was deliberate!" commented Sir Hugo, brushing snow from his shoulders with his free hand.

"Bad old bird!" shouted Penn, as he swung between his companions, and Amy laughed aloud, suddenly filled with joy at being alive on such a perfect day.

Hugo turned at the unexpected sound. "That's the first time you've done that," he was surprised into saying. "Laughed aloud, I mean."

Amy sobered instantly, the laughter dying from her eyes as she composed her features. "It is so long since I was on the ice that in my enjoyment I forgot that I was a young lady's companion."

"Then forget again," was the prompt reply, but recalled to her position, the moment had gone and Amy could not recapture her artless pleasure.

Shortly after that they turned back and once at the fallen log, Sir Hugo divested Penn of his skates, despite the child's loud protests. Throwing himself in the snow, howling with all his might, he refused to stand on his feet and after a moment Sir Hugo tucked his ward under his arm and set off back to the house, ignoring his wild struggles.

"Penn—Penn, you are behaving dreadfully," Amy told him, almost having to run to keep up with Sir Hugo's long strides.

"Behave," he ordered and administered a sharp slap to the conveniently upturned seat of Penn's nankeen trousers. "If you behave like a baby, I shall think you much too young to skate again," he warned, and, after a moment's thought, Penn let his sobs die away into loud hiccups. "Good. Now, I am sure you will walk beside us like a gentleman," and the boy was placed on his feet.

As Penn scrubbed at his face with his sleeve, Amy silently proffered her handkerchief, ignoring the pair of eyes that rolled dolefully at them both.

"Blow your nose," she advised helpfully, "or you will arrive home with an icicle on the end!"

A reluctant, rather soggy chuckle shook the small figure, and, restored to cheerfulness, he ran ahead as the adults exchanged glances of amusement.

"He's a game little fellow," said his uncle, watching him charge through the snow.

"He's a dear little boy," responded Amy warmly and looked up to discover that she was being studied with interest. Something in his gaze made her flush and, suddenly aware that much of her hair had escaped from the strict confines she usually imposed upon it and now hung around her face in curling elfin-locks, she did her best to tuck it back under her bonnet and restore the severe image she cultivated.

"I am glad you feel able to leave off your spectacles," remarked Sir Hugo inconsequentially and hurried on as Amy struggled to think of some reply. "The skates—impress upon Penn not to visit the river alone. In fact it would be best if the skates were put out of reach and sight and then we need have no cause to worry that he will be tempted." Having reached the house, he sketched a salute and flicked Penn's rosy cheek with one finger before leaving them at the door.

To everyone's intense relief, the deep cold continued unabated. The day of Clarissa's eagerly awaited party dawned bright and clear and the whole household, save his lordship, who closeted himself behind the closed door of his study, threw itself into the preparations, most of which could only be done on the day itself. A trestled table was set up; the lighting of the bonfire, over which a side of beef was to be roasted, was superintended by Mr. Hodge, the head gardener, and Mr. Hill, who had been spared from the kitchen by his overwrought spouse, took it upon himself to oversee the final arrangements in the pavilion, while the busy cook wondered if there was any means of removing Mrs. Hill from her domain without irreversibly ruining their relationship.

An early, cold collation had been arranged for the family to keep the pangs of hunger at bay until the guests had arrived and the soup, beef, and hot patties and potatoes were ready to consume. Torches were lit and placed in strategic places, and at last the rumble of wheels heralded the arrival of the first guests.

Clarissa, who with the other ladies had been hovering in the hall, danced out onto the steps to greet them and take them along the cleared path to the river, where Sir Hugo and Lucius awaited them. Quickly more guests arrived and groups were formed; soon the ice was covered by exuberant people. Happy shouts and laughter filled the air. A magnificent moon had risen, flooding the scene with brilliant, silvery light, and mindful of having supported Clarissa when she needed her, Amy felt free to collect the delicacies she had promised Penn.

"Cold and exercise are great appetizers," murmured a voice in her ear and, turning, she found

89

Sir Hugo viewing her laden plate with an uplifted eyebrow. "I take it that you have promised to keep my nephew from starvation," he added, taking pity on her confusion as she tried to think of some way of explaining her action without implicating the small boy.

"He has promised to go to sleep as soon as he has eaten it," she assured him.

"I am only surprised that Miss James has allowed it," Sir Hugo returned and she was silent, thinking herself reprimanded. Reading her expression, he hastened to reassure her. "I remember when I was a child, Cousin—you had best go quickly about your business and hope that she will remain unaware of such nefarious activities."

"And that Penn's digestion will cope—Good God!" Behind his lordship a young man had just strolled into view, gallant in dashing regimentals, the cold moonlight serving to heighten his resemblance to a statue of a Greek god.

Turning, Sir Hugo followed her gaze and smiled slightly. "Precisely so," he agreed. "What chance had Clarissa, when her childhood friend blossomed into such beauty!"

"Men have no right to look like that," Amy stated with conviction, studying the golden curls that clustered on the lofty brow, the aquiline nose, the chiseled mouth and cheekbones.

To his credit, Kit Masters appeared unaware of his good looks, attending to the ladies on either arm with good humor and greeting friends without condescension or arrogance.

"Take Penn his treat—I must attend to my guests," said Sir Hugo, aware that Clarissa had seen the Masters family and was advancing upon them with all speed. He arrived just before her and was able to control her first greeting by a repressive look. "Mrs. Masters, Miss Sarah—how pleasant that you could join us," he said easily before turning to the young man. "I am glad to see you home safe and well, Kit. How long are you on furlough?"

Slipping away as he exchanged pleasantries, Amy quickly returned to the house, which seemed strangely deserted, and made her way up the stairs to Penn's room. She found the little boy kneeling on the window seat, gazing longingly down at the flickering lights below.

"Ssh!" With one finger against her lips, she urged him to silence as he turned at her entrance. "We must not disturb Miss James," she whispered, bending to feel the cold, bare feet sticking out from under his nightshirt. "Oh, Penn, you are frozen. Could you not have at least worn your slippers?" Taking the quilt from his bed, she wrapped it round him, tucking his icy feet into its folds. "See what I have brought you."

Settling him on her lap, she presented the plate, smiling as he examined it solemnly, bending forward to make his selection. Choosing a square of sticky gingerbread, he bit into it and leaned contentedly back against her as he munched blissfully. His soft hair tickled her chin and, overcome by a surge of love, she hugged him to her. Reaching round, he planted a moist, sticky kiss on her cheek before turning back to the important business of disposing of his goodies.

Midway through a roast apple stuffed with dried fruit and cinnamon, he fell asleep, his head heavy against her chest and, holding him carefully, Amy rose to her feet and carried him back to bed. Tucking the bedclothes about him, she gazed down at his sleeping face for a moment before dropping a kiss on his smooth cheek. She then crept from the room, careful to take all evidence of the illicit feast with her.

"Oh, Aunt Almeria, there you are!" Clarissa greeted her upon her return. She brought forward the plump, retiring maiden of some sixteen years whom Amy had seen on Lieutenant Masters's arm. "This is my dearest Kit's sister, Sarah."

Amy smiled at the younger girl and made conversation until the chance arose to take Clarissa aside. "I daresay you may have forgotten that it is not considered at all the thing to refer to a gentleman, to whom one is not related, with terms of endearment. I mention this as I am quite sure you would not wish to appear gauche, or be thought beyond the pale," she said, her voice severe.

Clarissa flushed, but shrugged her shoulders. "Pooh! What do I care for convention!"

"*You* may not—but I have a very good idea that Lieutenant Masters does!" Amy returned shrewdly and knew she had been right when her charge frowned and said nothing, instead studying the toe of her bronze kid boot with great interest.

Two gentlemen strolled out of the shadows toward them and Amy recognized Sir Hugo and Lieutenant Shovell. Seeing the man she had come to believe her savior, Clarissa brightened and started forward, her hand out.

"How pleased I am that you have come," she said with all of the charm of which she was capable, her annoyance forgotten. "Let me introduce you to my friend, Miss Sarah Masters. Sarah, this is Lieutenant Shovell, of whom I have spoken."

As the younger girl curtsied, the naval man bowed, but looked puzzled. "There is some mistake—" he began.

"Indeed so. You have the name wrong, Clarissa," put in her brother smoothly, a hint of malicious amusement in his voice. "This is Sir Simon Lovell."

Clarissa gasped and her eyes widened as she gazed at the lieutenant, unable to conceal the horror she felt.

"Do forgive us for saddling you with the wrong name," put in Amy quickly, stepping between her charge and the sailor. "Tell me, have you seen that young ragamuffin we rescued since? Or any sign of his would-be abductor?"

Lieutenant Lovell shook his head. "I took the precaution of calling in to inform the beadle of the happening, but the gang of pickpockets and beggars seems to have left the district."

"I vow I am bored with the whole thing! Such an old story, I must have told it a hundred times," cried Clarissa, having made a good recovery from her shock. She spoke lightly but her voice was dangerously high and she sent her brother a darkling look from under her eyelashes. "Sir Simon, pray take me onto the ice—I am sure my brother will have no objection to you as a partner."

With a bland gesture, Sir Hugo stepped back and shortly the lieutenant and Clarissa were besporting themselves creditably on the ice.

"That was not well done," Amy could not forbear from saying, following her employer's gaze as he watched the couple.

"No, indeed not," he agreed promptly. "I am

quite ashamed of myself! Clarissa needed a lesson—now she knows that, far from being an elderly suitor foisted upon her without regard to her age, Sir Simon is eminently suitable. She, herself, was in transports about him—"

"Until she was told his name so brutally," Amy returned. "Now she will be embarrassed at the thought of her mistake—I only hope her temper may not lead her into some indiscretion, for she is very angry with you."

"That is why I employed you, Miss Standish," Sir Hugo said levelly and Amy heard her name, which had grown unfamiliar during the previous weeks, with a sense of shock. "I leave her in your care—Cousin. My advice would be to keep an eye on her."

With a brief nod, he sauntered away—leaving her in no doubt that he considered her to have overstepped the bounds of her position. The next time Amy saw him, he was partnering Mrs. Masters upon the ice.

"Please, Miss Almeria." As a hand touched her arm tentatively, Amy turned to see Sarah Masters eyeing her with a beseeching gaze. "I—do not feel well," she whispered, her voice weak and tremulous.

After a comprehensive look, taking in her hot cheeks and unnaturally bright eyes and the way she hugged her arms around her shivering body, Amy drew her into the pavilion, seated her in a chair, and wrapped her own shawl about her shoulders. She left her in the ready care of Miss Witherspoon who had ensconced herself in the shelter, preferring to view the proceedings in comfort and comparative warmth. Presenting the girl with a cup of hot fruit punch and enjoining her to drink it, Amy went in search of Mrs. Masters.

Sir Hugo was now partnering a rather dashing widow, their prowess so skillful that a space around them had been cleared and they were encircled by an admiring group. At last Amy came upon Mrs. Masters seated on a log beside the bonfire, being waited upon by an attentive Sir Simon Lovell, and quickly made known her errand.

"I rather suspected this might happen!" exclaimed Sarah's mother, handing her plate to the lieutenant and jumping to her feet. "She was not herself this morning and should have cried off, but she would come—this is her first grown-up party, Miss Standish."

"I quite understand," said Amy soothingly, leading the way. "Life is so intense at that age, is it not?"

A drooping Miss Masters burst into tears at the sight of her mother. "Oh, Mama!" she cried. "I feel so horrid! I'm cold and the lights hurt my head and it is so n-noisy—and I wish I was at home."

"So you shall be, my pet, just as soon as we can manage it," her mother told her, gathering her into her arms, feeling her burning head with one hand. Above Sarah's head, she looked at Amy with mute appeal.

"I sent a servant to have your coach made ready," she responded quietly. "Shall I fetch Kit?"

"No—the poor boy has little enough time to enjoy himself before he goes back to France—"

"Let me," offered Lieutenant Lovell, and without further ado and in a competent manner that won Amy's instant approval, he scooped Miss Sarah into his arms and bore her off toward the house.

95

When Amy returned, charged with apologies to the host and explanations for Kit, it slowly dawned on her, with growing dismay, that the two young people were not to be found among the throng of guests; not only could she not find Kit Masters to deliver his mother's message, but Clarissa appeared to have vanished without trace. Her last hope faded when she saw Lucius partnering some unknown maiden, though, truly, she hardly expected Clarissa to be skating with her cousin.

"Exactly," said a voice at her elbow, as she stood on tiptoe the better to search the happy throng. "I have been seeking for my sister these last ten minutes."

"I daresay that she has returned to the house for some reason," Amy returned, keeping her voice as calm and unconcerned as possible. "I am sure you need have no fear. Lieutenant Masters struck me as an eminently sensible young man."

"I hope you are right," the baronet said ominously. "Come, Cousin, take a turn on the ice with me, we cannot be seen in a bother."

With one arm around her waist and her hand in a firm grasp, Sir Hugo guided her along the gliding, pirouetting couples. More disturbed by the closeness of his body than she cared to admit, Amy did her best to match his steps with equilibrium, conscious that many glances were being cast in their direction, not least by Lucius Gambrill.

"I'll lay wager that they are concealed in the old arbor," murmured a voice in her ear. "It would be the very place that my ninny-headed sister would think romantic! Only she would think a rotting garden ruin would be the place for an assignation!" With that thought, he lengthened his stride purposefully, skating out of the wide part of the river, encircled by flaring torches, and sped along a narrow, unfrequented stretch of ice.

Taking his action as a suggestion of some new diversion, the guests fell in behind, following the two leading figures, pair by pair. The thought of the disaster ahead for the errant pair, should they be discovered closeted together in the arbor, was borne upon Amy, knowing as she did that gossip had ruined many a young lady's chance of a good marriage. If only there was some way of warning her charge of their approach, she thought, and out of sheer despair she did the only thing possible and began to sing loudly as the dark bulk of the old building on the bank of the river came into sight.

Lifting her voice in the only song she could think of, which happened to be "Come Lasses and Lads," she heard with relief the couples behind join in the old song that, by happy chance, lent itself to the swinging motion of skating.

A pale blur that could only be a face appeared cautiously in the dark entrance, a smaller one below it. For a moment they hung there as if enchanted and then, as the singing procession drew near, Amy was relieved to see them disappear.

"Well done, Cousin," murmured Sir Hugo. "Now we have just to extricate them—" Leading the string of skaters so that they lost their precise placing and became a laughing gaggle, he glided close to the arbor and, by some skill unimagined by Amy, scooped up Clarissa and Kit Masters in passing. Quite how it was managed, Amy had no idea, but on the way back to the fire she found herself being partnered by the lieutenant, while Clarissa was in her brother's firm grasp.

97

Amy did not hear what Sir Hugo said to Kit, but it was a very chastened young man who bid them all good night. Clarissa was by her brother's side as their guests took their leave, but from her white face and tense expression, Amy knew that her composure would not outlast the final guest.

"I expected better of you," Sir Hugo said coldly when they were alone, and, forestalling any outburst, turned to leave the hall. "I will see you both after breakfast tomorrow," he added with an unkind look divided between his sister and her companion.

CHAPTER SIX

Seeing the signs of imminent rage and hysteria, Amy declined recriminations. Instead she escorted her charge upstairs and, with great practicality, set about putting her to bed, having dismissed the maid. This treatment had the effect of cooling Clarissa's temper and tears formed in her blue eyes and began to fall dramatically.

"Yes, very well done," said Miss Standish calmly, "but remember that you have told me that you can do that at will and so your tears will have little effect on me."

"Oh, Aunt Almeria—what can he have said to my poor Kit?" cried Clarissa, abandoning her tears. "I have never seen him so cast down, almost *crushed*, and to have gone home without a word to me!"

"Perhaps he thought it for the best," was her companion's prosaic suggestion as she folded the other's discarded clothing.

"When it may be the last time we meet!" was Clarissa's dramatic response. "We shall be torn apart!"

"Really?" Miss Standish looked interested. "I quite thought such things only happened on the stage, but I daresay that you know better than I!"

"I h-had hoped for some k-kindness and understanding, from you at least. You are not sympathetic!"

"No, indeed," agreed Amy readily. "Which is not to be wondered at, for your action has very like put me in danger of losing my position. Sir Hugo can hardly be regarding me as a servant worthy of hire!"

"Oh!" Clarissa exclaimed in dismay, her eyes wide with contrition. "Oh, Aunt Almeria! I will tell him it was nothing to do with you—"

"Nevertheless, I should have seen—have been aware—indeed, I *was* aware of the likely effect that the episode of Lieutenant Lovell's name would have upon someone of your temperament."

"My wretched brother," muttered Clarissa through her teeth. "I wish never to see him again!"

"A wish unlikely to be granted," pointed out her companion, "for we both have an appointment with him first thing tomorrow."

Fresh tears appeared in Clarissa's eyes and she bit her knuckles to keep back a sob. Seeing that she was truly miserable and not merely indulging herself in order to engender sympathy, Amy made a proposal; and so it was she who descended to the study first next morning, despite Sir Hugo having sent for his sister.

As she entered, he was standing in the window embrasure staring out across the snow-covered park, and she saw that he was dressed for riding in blue coat and buckskin breeches, his black Hessian boots so highly polished that they reflected the flames from the fire. He did not turn at once, but left her to wait for a few uncomfortable moments before acknowledging her presence. Seeing Amy instead of Clarissa, he frowned, his grim expression unaltered.

"You are mistaken; I sent for my sister," he said icily, his eyes glittering like chips of jet.

"I hoped that you would see me first," she said, determined not to be made nervous by his intimidating gaze. "I would be grateful if you would let me explain."

"There is nothing to explain, Miss Standish, and certainly no excuses to be made for my sister's behavior—or your lack of control over her. I expected her to be safe under your care; instead I find her running wild and endangering her reputation, when I have engaged you to control her youthful excesses."

"I have no excuse, sir, for my own lack of action. I admit that I should have taken better care of Clarissa and, indeed, would have done if Sarah Masters had not fallen ill and needed my attention." She paused to take a steadying breath before going on. "But you yourself are much to blame for her actions, as you must be aware!" She held her breath as his mouth tightened and he grew pale with suppressed fury, hurrying on before he could speak. "Have you no notion how she must have felt when she discovered that her heroic lieutenant was none other than her despised suitor? At that age, sir, you must know that nothing is so painful as to be made to feel stupid!"

"I must confess that *I* had not expected to be lectured, ma'am," Sir Hugo remarked, gazing at her down the length of his aquiline nose. "I would advise you to have a care. You are doing your own somewhat precarious position no good at all."

Amy bit her lip, longing to sink into a chair, yet

not able to do so without some gesture from her employer who, she had a very good notion, kept her standing in order to emphasize the lowliness of her position. Bending her head, she stared at the rug beneath her feet until the silence grew oppressive. "I feel sure that you cannot be aware that Clarissa holds you in some fear," she said baldly at last, coming to the crux of what she wished to say.

When he did not reply, she glanced up to find him staring at her, his expression that of a man struck by astonishment, and she ventured to go on. "I am convinced that a man of your intelligence has no need to rule by fear—even if Clarissa was not fond of you, other ways to manage her could be found. She is not biddable, but readily affectionate, and it would only be wise to use this trait."

"Indeed." Sir Hugo swung abruptly away from the window, gesturing to her to be seated, and took the chair opposite. Leaning back, he regarded her coolly, his long fingers drumming against the wooden arm. "So, you would tell me how to manage my own family. How fortunate for us all that I chanced upon you in that inn!"

Ignoring the irony in his voice, Amy returned his gaze as steadily as she was able, willing to fight for the happiness of her charge. "Clarissa would respond better to kindness than the goad," she told him.

"Nonsense! If you think that Miss Witherspoon even *thought* of applying a goad, then let me tell you, Miss Standish, that *you* are not as sharp as I've taken you to be."

"I've no doubt that Miss Witherspoon is both good and kind—but those are the very things that serve to irritate Clarissa into behaving badly."

"Eating your words, ma'am?" he asked with a rise of his eyebrows. "You have just told me that Clarissa needs kindness and now you say she finds Miss Witherspoon's kindness annoying. You cannot have it both ways. To return to last night, I would remind you that I was not *kind* when I did nothing to correct her hearing of Sir Simon's name."

"No, indeed," Amy agreed with composure. "You were behaving badly!"

There was a moment's astonished silence and Amy wondered if she had gone too far, before the man opposite gave a harsh bark of laughter.

"Touché," he acknowledged. "Well then, Cousin, be pleased to give me your advice—though I give no promise to take it. I undertake only to listen."

Realizing by his use of the familiar title that his mood had softened slightly, Amy gathered her forces, knowing that this was her chance to ease the fraught situation between brother and sister. "Clarissa holds you in admiration and affection—"

"Then let me tell you, ma'am, that she hides her emotion very well! The wretched girl has done nothing but her best to thwart me at every turn. If I were to suggest she wear pink, which is her favorite color, she would immediately deck herself in blue—if I propose an outing to Astley's to see the equine spectacle, she would affect a headache—"

"I am sure you exaggerate," interposed Amy, "for I have heard her often say how she longed to visit the horse circus."

"Perhaps—exaggeration is very easily entered into when dealing with my ninny-headed sibling."

"She misses Julian very much," Amy said quietly.

Gray eyes regarded her. "She never mentions

him. . . . I supposed her too flighty to care. No emotion has a deep effect upon her. In fact, I have long thought her of a somewhat shallow disposition."

"You do her an injustice, Sir Hugo. She has had no experience of life. Miss Witherspoon, while no doubt a good teacher of schoolroom subjects, has not the nature or experience herself to introduce her pupil to deeper thoughts."

Sir Hugo gave her a wintery smile. "I do not believe Clarissa capable of deeper thinking," he commented dryly. "She is a charming muttonhead, like her mother."

"She is very attached to Penn."

"Penn has the ability to attract affection—as, I think, you have found."

"Y-yes," she answered, aware of being scrutinized by his gray eyes. "He is a dear little boy."

"A little imp, with all the charm of his grandmama."

"Grandmother?" She looked up sharply, surprised into thinking for one moment that he was alluding to her own mother.

"Julian and Clarissa's mother—to whom else would I refer?"

"He must have had a mother, and so another set of relatives," she was stung into replying.

"Of course," Sir Hugo acknowledged, his drawl much in evidence. "An actress of no merit, who inveigled Julian into wedlock—she can have bequeathed Penn nothing save a certain cunning and guile."

"You are very hard."

"Clorinda Beaufort—for such was the aristocratic name she went under—a female of uncertain morals and little compunction, set herself out to

104

trap a youth, still wet behind the ears and easily besotted by good looks and artifice, into an unsuitable marriage."

Amy was silent, knowing that her sister had done precisely that. Chloe had made no bones about the "callow boy" who was in thrall to her, laughing at his protestations of love and declaring that she *would* have him, even if he did not bring a title with his marriage lines. "But, Mama, *such* wealth!" she had exclaimed to her shocked mother, and marry Julian Dysart she did, despite her own family's opposition.

"Do you know Penn's maternal family?" she could not stop herself asking, despite knowing that to bring up that particular subject could not be wise. "Perhaps they are not too unsuitable."

"They will be like the odious Clorinda—commonplace shysters, hoping to live off my brother's wealth. Bloodsuckers, thinking only to advance themselves by leeching onto a youth who was innocent enough to think to marry a high-flyer rather than to make her his mistress. I paid the woman off and since have done my best to ensure that everyone forgets that Penn came from such a lineage!"

"But to cut them off with such finality! To let them have no contact—to make Penn forget the existence of that side of his family cannot be right!" she burst out passionately, goaded into unwary speech by anger at his scorn. "What heartache you have caused—" She broke off, struggling to regain control of her emotions.

"You speak as if you know these unworthy people," remarked Sir Hugo slowly, his expression thoughtful.

"No, no—how could I?" Amy cried. "But I do know how my mother longs to see *her* grandchild."

"Why should she not?" inquired her employer.

"There—are family reasons. We are estranged."

"How unfortunate," he mused. "But in this case, Penn's mother was only too willing to accept a settlement and hand her son over to my absolute care." He paused and again Amy was aware of a shrewd scrutiny. "Tell me, Cousin, how did you know these details? It is an old story and one not readily known outside of the family."

"I—cannot remember." Amy injected a puzzled note into her voice, hoping to cover her mistake in allowing her feelings to betray her knowledge. "Someone must have mentioned it in conversation." By his expression she knew that Sir Hugo was unconvinced by this explanation, and she hurried on as if the matter was of little importance to her. "May I give you my apologies for not taking better care of Clarissa? I am sure nothing like it will happen again; if only she could be convinced of the affection in which, I am certain, you hold her, she would be a happier girl. To be thought unloved, you know, makes for wildness."

A cold gaze seemed to bore through her and she had no way of telling if her plea had made any impression or not. After a moment, he told her quietly to send his sister to him, his expression implacable, and with a little sigh of frustration, she obeyed.

Sometime later, Clarissa burst into the parlor, her face alight. "Of all the things!" she cried. "I vow it is beyond imagining—I expected Hugo to read me one of his famous scolds, and I quite acknowledge that I deserved it, for to own the truth, he had put me in such a rage that I would have run away with the music master, if one had been available! My brother hardly mentioned my misdemeanor of last night, but talked of my dearest Julian and even made an apology for letting me carry on with my mistaking of Sir Simon's name! Sometimes Hugo can be beyond all understanding." She seated herself at the little inlaid desk, sending Amy a roguish look over her shoulder. "And now, Aunt Almeria, my fierce, stern brother has agreed that common politeness dictates that I should write to Mrs. Masters, inquiring upon the health of my dearest Sarah!" And with a little sigh of pleasure, she set herself to the task.

After a while Amy grew tired of watching her charge scribble a few lines only to screw up the paper and throw it aside in order to start anew, and took herself off with the idea of looking in upon Penn. Greatly to her surprise, the schoolroom was empty. Paper and ink lay discarded on the table where her nephew had obviously been practicing his pothooks yet again, but of Penn and his governess there was no sign. Finding the bedroom empty, too, Amy crossed the landing to knock upon Miss James's door. When she received no answer beyond a faint, genteel snore, she opened it and peered in, spying the recumbent form of the governess fully clothed upon the bed, her eyes closed and her bosom rising and falling gently. She failed to respond to her name, not rousing, even when Amy seized her shoulders and shook them, beyond muttering unintelligibly and settling her head more comfortably into the pillows.

Puzzled, Amy bent nearer to the sleeping face and drew back as a sweetish, flowerlike smell carried to her nostrils. Unable to recognize it, she frowned, considering her next move. Penn could be anywhere in the house, or with a servant or member of the family, but a faint foreboding, not much more than unease, bothered her and she returned to the nursery, searching quickly until she was certain that the child's outdoor clothes were missing, too.

It did not take her long to return to the parlor to instruct a startled Clarissa that Penn appeared to be missing and that a search of the house should be organized while she, herself, ran quickly to the river to make certain that the ice had not attracted him there.

She snatched up a cloak as she hurried through the hall and wrapped it about her shoulders as she ran along the path so many had traversed the night before. Her thin slippers and stockings were soon soaked through, making her realize with growing concern that a thaw had set in overnight and the snow was swiftly melting. Arriving at the scene of last night's entertainment, she crossed the trampled snow, skirted the wet, black mess of the remains of the bonfire, and spared a quick glance round the empty pavilion before reluctantly turning to the river. At first she thought this was deserted, too, and her heart rose, until, venturing out onto the ice, the better to view each direction, she caught a glimpse of something bright red before it rounded a bend and vanished from sight. That particular color was so unnatural in that bleak, black-and-white landscape that she knew it could only be Penn's scarlet wool scarf and she started off in pursuit.

A thin covering of water sat on the ice, making it doubly hard to keep her footing, and she fell several times in her sliding, gliding, precarious attempt to catch up with the boy. Soon she discarded the long cloak, the long wet folds of which wrapped themselves round her, entangling her legs and adding to her difficulties.

"Penn, Penn," she called despairingly, her voice sounding eerie and desolate in the silence.

Rounding the bend in an ignominious flurry of uncontrolled movement, she saw her quarry ahead, and even in that moment she noticed that he was skating with a surprising degree of competence. Hearing his name, he glanced over his shoulder, giving her a wide, mischievous grin as he put on a spurt of speed. At that moment a figure hurtled out of the bushes that lined the bank and sped across the ice to collide violently with Amy. As they both fell heavily, Amy just had time to see another form detach itself from the bank and a long arm reach out to catch the unsuspecting Penn, whose attention was riveted on the extraordinary spectacle behind him.

The ice cracked under the sudden weight of their bodies and just before black, freezing water closed over her head, Amy recognized the man who flung Penn to the safety of the bank as Sir Hugo. Fright and cold made her struggle free from the grasp of her unknown attacker, who appeared to be clutching at her in a frenzy, and suddenly her feet found the uneven bottom of the river. Straightening her legs, she found to her surprise that she could stand up, the water reaching only halfway up her chest.

With a wild heaving and gurgling, Lucius rose beside her, his eyes closed and his mouth wide in an unintelligible scream as he thrashed madly at the ice and water around him.

Ducking under one wildly flailing arm, Amy dealt him a smart box on the ear, which served to cut off his yells and make him open his eyes. "You can *wade* to the bank!" she shouted at him, trying to keep herself upright against the tow of the river.

"Take my hand," commanded a voice from nearby, and turning her head, she saw that Sir Hugo had spread-eagled himself on the remaining solid ice and was stretching his arm toward her.

Their hands met and he exerted a steady pull, drawing her toward him, breaking and pushing aside the ice, until he could kneel upright and drag her out of the water. Leaving her for a minute, he reached back and, catching the still-floundering Lucius by the collar of his coat, heaved him out to join her on the bank.

Shivering so violently that her legs refused to support her, Amy crawled on her hands and knees away from the river, the soft snow no colder than her hands, which she noticed had assumed an unusual purplish shade. By this time a string of servants had arrived, headed by James Fifield, and commanding him to take charge of Penn and have a care for his gasping and sputtering cousin, Sir Hugo tore off his coat and wrapped Amy in it before, scooping her up, he tossed her over his shoulder in a most ungentlemanly way and set off back to the house.

With her head dangling down his back, she clutched at his coat, each step her rescuer took jolting her abdomen against his shoulder and forcing out her breath in the most uncomfortable way.

"P-put—me—down!" she cried, rearing upright, only to have him tighten his grasp on her knees

110

and, ignoring her appeal, make more speed toward the Manor.

Shouting for Mrs. Hill the moment they arrived in the hall, he then charged up the stairs, apparently thinking Amy incapable of walking. Raising her head, she had a brief glimpse of Clarissa's astonished face peering out from a doorway before a confused array of wooden banisters, polished stair-treads, and wide floorboards passed in quick succession under her nose as she was borne up to her bedchamber.

Setting her on her feet, he supported her with one hand and began to unbutton her jacket with the other. The wet material was unyielding and he released her, the better to attack the stubborn buttonholes. Amy's legs folded under her and for a moment, she hung suspended by her spencer, before her weight unbalanced Sir Hugo and they both toppled to the floor.

The housekeeper and Clarissa arrived in time to find Sir Hugo apparently fighting with a decidedly wet and disheveled Miss Standish, in what appeared to be an attempt to tear off her clothes.

"My Lord!" cried Mrs. Hill in outraged tones, frozen in the doorway, her black-clad figure rigid with indignation.

Brought to a realization of how his actions must appear, Sir Hugo released Amy and climbed to his knees. "Ah, Mrs. Hill, there you are," he said, with an assumption of ease, as he rose to his feet. "Pray be so good as to give Miss Standish a hot bath." And with a pleasant bow, directed impartially toward all three women, he left the room, whistling softly.

Two pairs of round, astonished eyes were turned

111

upon Amy, who was sitting on the floor, soaked skirts above her knees, displaying an inordinate length of shapely leg. Wet hair had released itself from its confining plaits and hung in wild curls and tendrils about her shoulders. A frond of slimy, brown waterweed was draped elegantly over one eyebrow and she removed it with care before, meeting the petrified gazes fixed upon her, she broke into whoops of laughter.

All was soon explained and a thoroughly warmed and dried Miss Standish tucked into bed with the comfort of a hot posset prepared to the house-keeper's own recipe. An occasional chuckle shook her and Clarissa had only to catch her eye for them both to break into renewed giggles.

"Why Mr. Gambrill felt called upon to hurl him-self at me in that way, I h-have no idea, but it was certainly spectacular!" Amy said, recalling the cause of the accident.

"Lucius tells me that he saw the ice cracking fur-ther along and hoped to save you. *I* think him quite heroic!" Clarissa returned, surprising Amy with her defense of her cousin. "*Hugo* did not even get wet! Well—only with the water he shared with you. How very fit he must be to carry you from the river . . . though I must own that to throw one over his shoulder is not precisely *romantic*!"

"Oh, dear!" sighed Amy, leaning back against her pillows, feeling her cheeks glowing with embarrass-ment. "How shall I face him at dinner?"

"No need to bother about that—for he has taken himself off on some urgent business with Sir Si-mon!" Clarissa assured her, smothering another giggle. "So you will only have Lucius and Mr. Fifield to contend with. I promise that Withy and I

112

shall be the souls of discretion and n-never m-mention water or the river."

Looking at her dancing eyes, Amy wondered doubtfully if her self-control could be counted on but found later, as she had known she would, that James Fifield was kindness itself, his calm good manners putting her immediately at ease when he met her in the hall that evening. Suspecting that he had been waiting for her, she accepted his arm and allowed him to take her in to dinner. Clarissa and Lucius, who had been in conversation in front of the fire, turned at their entrance and, to Amy, it appeared that the fair man bore himself with an air of stoic martyrdom.

"Mr. Gambrill," she said, going forward. "How glad I am to see that you took no ill effects from our adventure this morning. I really believe that Penn had a surfeit of rescuers!"

"It was unfortunate that you did not heed my shout. From where I was, it was clear that your weight was causing the ice to fracture. The nearer you approached to Penn, the more danger he was in."

Amy frowned in perplexity. "I did not see any cracks," she said.

"I had a better view—and was forced to take the only course I saw to save the child's life. Really, Miss Standish, it was very remiss of you to let him get so far ahead. . . . I will not mention the unwiseness of taking him out upon the ice in such conditions!"

"No, indeed, do not," she returned steadily, "for I did no such thing. I found Penn missing from the schoolroom and went in search of him."

Mr. Fifield looked up with sudden interest. "Miss James? . . ." he inquired delicately.

"Asleep," Amy explained briefly. "I could not waken her. Penn's outdoor clothes were gone—so I suspected where he might be. He had been very envious of our ice party and it took only a little thought to realize where he had gone."

"And the skates, Miss Standish? How did he get those?" asked Lucius Gambrill.

Recognizing the faint hint of maliciousness in his question, Amy regarded him thoughtfully. "I have no idea," she returned. "I put them on a shelf in the passage off the hall. It is much too high for him to reach, even if he knew they were there, which I am sure he did not."

Mr. Gambrill looked disbelieving, but Miss Witherspoon entered at that moment and the matter was forgotten in her flurry of nervous inquiries and excited exclamations.

Next morning, eager to be sure that her nephew had suffered no ill effects, Amy made her way up to the nursery before breakfast. As she entered the room, Miss James was bending over the bed in the act of spooning liquid into the small boy's mouth, and supposing it some kind of medicine, Amy would have taken little notice, if there had not been something furtive in the way in which the governess jumped and hastily returned the small vial to a cupboard and locked the door.

"Is he not well?" Amy asked, surprised to find Penn in bed and in need of medicine. "What a slugabed you are," she rallied him, going to his side as he moved his head fretfully on the pillow. Feeling his forehead with her hand, she was relieved to find it cool, but was disturbed that he appeared so

114

sleepy, his eyes heavy and almost unfocused. "What is wrong?" she asked anxiously.

"Penn is a little unwell this morning. His is a delicate disposition, as I am well aware. I have discovered that overexcitement brings on his headaches. There is no need to worry, Miss Standish, I am quite capable of dealing with his constitution. A day in bed and I have every hope of a complete recovery."

"And you, Miss James, are you quite recovered? Were you not well, yesterday, that you felt the need to take to your bed?"

"I lay down for the merest minute," the governess replied, defending herself.

"Long enough for Penn to put himself in danger," Amy pointed out. "It was by the slightest chance that I happened to come up here. I would remind you that had I not, he would very like have been in serious danger."

Miss James looked away, muttering disjointedly about migraines and leaving her charge well provided with tasks to keep him occupied. "And, really, you know, he was well aware that he should not leave the room," she finished, adding somewhat defiantly that all the attention he was receiving was not good for one of his nervous disposition.

"The woman talked as if he were an invalid!" Amy told Clarissa later. "A little boy should not have 'a nervous disposition' and headaches as if they were a regular thing." She brooded darkly for a moment. "And what," she asked, thoughtfully, "does she dose him with?"

"Mrs. Hill will know," Clarissa told her. "She is the one who hands out any medicine other than whatever Dr. Frazer dispenses."

But the housekeeper shook her head when questioned. "Master Penn's taking nothing of mine," she declared, "and no harm it would do him, if he was! I can't say what that Miss James might give him. As governess, she's not under my jurisdiction." She set her lips, falling silent, while giving the impression that if she chose, she might say a great deal.

"Penn seems rather disposed to have the headache, does he not?" ventured Amy, hoping to encourage her into being indiscreet. Mrs. Hill snorted loudly in a disbelieving manner, but still said nothing and after a moment the other went on. "Which is strange, for he gives the appearance of being a robust child. However, Miss James does say that his chest is weak—"

"There's nothing wrong with his chest, bar a childish snuffle now and again, if you ask me," the housekeeper said suddenly. "My belief is that he is ill to Miss's convenience!"

Amy stared at the older woman. "What do you mean?" she asked.

Mrs. Hill played with her chatelaine, obviously wondering if she had been wise to say so much. Meeting Amy's eyes, she read the concern there and decided to take her into her confidence. "It's easy to put a child to bed—much easier than looking after a lively boy. And if he has a chest susceptible to the cold, then it is best to keep him in—especially if you don't care for walks yourself. An outing never did any harm is what I say, but Miss James is not one for walks and so on."

"She does seem to take excessive care of him," Amy agreed, and the housekeeper sniffed loudly. "And, yet," Amy went on, "he managed to escape

116

her vigilance yesterday and somehow found his skates ... which I am certain were out of his reach."

"You'd be surprised where boys can reach," remarked the other, a reminiscent smile crossing her face. "I'd be surprised at nothing a young imp of Satan could do."

"You think he might have got them himself?"

"Well, if no one gave them to him, which no one would, he must have, mustn't he? I'd swear that none of the servants would have aided him—too fond of him, they are."

"It's a mystery, then. Like this medicine Miss James was giving him," remarked Amy. "It was from a small vial—some clear, colorless liquid." She paused, before adding tentatively: "Like laudanum, perhaps."

Mrs. Hill gave her familiar snort. "Gin, more like," she said, forgetting to be cautious. "I can't see Miss James being downright wicked, which dosing with laudanum would be, but a drop of Mother's Ruin—now, she might think that quite different."

"She might, indeed," murmured Amy, recalling the faint, sweet smell that had hovered over the governess's recumbent form. "And just the thing to produce headaches, I'd say."

Realizing that in her position she could hardly go to Sir Hugo bearing tales, she resolved to spend as much time as possible with Penn, hoping that her presence and obvious suspicions, which she would make no effort to hide, would have the effect of preventing any further dosing with gin.

CHAPTER SEVEN

With the thaw, news of events outside Candover Magna came to the house, and travel was possible once more. Sir Hugo and Mr. Fifield returned to London, intent upon attending to neglected business, and almost with their departure, it became obvious that the long-drawn-out fight between Britain and France must be drawing to a conclusion. Knowing that it could only be a matter of days before Kit Masters felt called upon to rejoin his regiment, Amy watched Clarissa for signs of anxiety, but her charge, who never read the newspapers, appeared to remain blithely unaware of the impending events.

The two younger ladies were studying the latest edition of *The Lady's Journal* with avid interest, while Miss Witherspoon was nursing a cold in her room, when the steady trot of approaching horses made them break off their conversation and exchange inquiring glances.

"Who can it be?" wondered Clarissa as the doorbell jangled imperiously. Unable to control her curiosity, she jumped to her feet and ran to the window. "Why!" she exclaimed, her voice a mixture of joy and puzzlement, craning her neck the better to peer below, "I do believe that is Kit's old charger being led away. I'd know Captain anywhere. What can have brought Kit here? Surely poor Sarah cannot be worse. She seemed on the mend when we visited."

Amy thought that she had a good idea as to the likely cause of the soldier's unexpected call, but said nothing, wishing that Sir Hugo had been at home to deal with this sudden difficulty. When the butler announced "Lieutenant Masters," in impassive tones, his face carefully blank, and the young man entered impetuously, Amy felt her heart sink. Kit was arrayed in all the glory of his regimentals, a masculine vision in red coat and gold braid, his black shako held against his chest, his sword swinging in a particularly dashing way against his hip.

A curl fell across his brow as he bowed, making Amy feel that he could not have managed it better if he had arranged it, and yet, to give him his due, he seemed completely oblivious of his appearance.

"I come to bid you farewell," he announced dramatically, and for a moment Amy wondered if she was watching a play. "I leave for London this afternoon—events in France make it imperative that I rejoin my regiment with all possible speed."

"Oh, *Kit*!" wailed Clarissa, joining in with relish. "Are we to be parted?" Advancing step by step across the room, she gave him both her hands, in a gesture worthy of a tragedy queen.

Miss Standish could not forbear clapping, and recalled to their surroundings, the young couple sprang apart.

"Oh, well *done*," she applauded. "I declare that Drury Lane is nowhere near as good—I can't quite name the play, however. . . ."

"Aunt Almeria, how can you be so—so—" Clarissa searched for a word, finally declaring that she was saddened to find her aunt so lacking in sensibility.

"Miss Standish," began Kit, searching in his pocket, his ears burning with embarrassment. Producing a slip of folded paper, he presented it to her with commendable composure. "The recipe Mama promised you—horehound and honey, for coughs, I believe."

"How kind of you to bring it—under the circumstances."

He smiled down at her in a way that made her realize his charm. "Under the circumstances—I was more than willing," he said. "I could not leave without seeing Clarissa. We have been friends since childhood, you know."

"Sir Hugo will be disappointed to have missed you," she said calmly and the boy frowned, recognizing her gentle warning.

"Is he not here? I had no idea that he was from home. I intended nothing underhand," he added boyishly.

Amy believed him. "I am sure Sir Hugo would have no objection to your paying us a call," she told him kindly. "How is Sarah? I hope she continues to improve."

"Yes, she does very well."

"And your mama—busy with her medicines and potions, I take it?"

"Mama enjoys her usual good health." He sent a look of entreaty to Clarissa, who turned a beseeching gaze upon Amy.

Taking pity upon them, she stood up, remarking lightly that if they would excuse her, she would pen

120

a reply to Mrs. Masters, and stepping into the window alcove, she seated herself at a little table half-hidden behind a curtain. As her pen scratched noisily across the paper, she was half aware of murmured conversation behind her, but allowed them what privacy she could by concentrating her attention on her letter. Signing it with her name, she shook sand over the ink and folded the paper, all her movements unusually noisy in order to warn the couple behind her that their tête-à-tête was about to be interrupted.

"There," she declared loudly, before turning back to the room. "I would be grateful if you would take that to your mother, Kit."

She saw that they had been standing very close together but the tall young man left Clarissa at once, coming to where Amy sat, half turned away from the little table.

Taking the folded paper, he made her a bow. "My thanks," he said simply, and she knew that he was not referring to the letter.

Looking up at him, her smile faltered as she involuntarily thought of the danger he was about to face. "Take care," she urged quietly.

"I will," he assured her, not pretending to misunderstand her, before he crossed the floor with a jangle of spurs and bent over Clarissa's hand, sketched them both a salute, and marched briskly out of the room.

As his footsteps died away, Clarissa awoke from her stricken trance and ran across to the window, crying brokenly: "Oh, my love—will I ever see you again?!"

"To be sure, you will," Miss Standish assured her briskly. "Now, Clarissa, such extravagances are all very well while we are alone, for I know that you are only funning, but I pray, do not allow yourself to fall into the way of playacting if anyone else should be present."

"Playacting!" exclaimed her charge in shocked tones. "Aunt Almeria, if I had known that you were so sadly in want of a little romantic sensibility when I chose you for an honorary aunt, I vow I would have thought again!"

Amy raised her eyebrows. "Would you indeed, most ungrateful of nieces! I daresay that if I had known that you intended to saddle me with such a name, *I* would have done the same thing!"

"Do you not care for it?" inquired Clarissa, distracted. "I think it rather romantic. I saw it in some book I read at school and decided straightaway that I would use it to name my daughter."

"And I am by way of being a trial run!" was her companion's heartfelt response. "Poor child—I pray you do no such thing, it could only have a reprehensible effect upon the girl. She would have no choice but to be thoroughly difficult and a sad trial to her family. I pity you such a daughter, Clarissa. I always hold that names have a great deal to answer for."

Abandoning her tears, Clarissa gave a chuckle. "I was wrong," she said, smiling at her companion. "I am glad that I found you. Withy is the dearest, kindest person, but she has never made me laugh, which you, dearest Aunt, quite often do!"

Amy contrived to look modest. "It is my only talent," she admitted, which caused her charge to give another gurgle of laughter.

"I remember terming you 'my only hope,'" she said, reminiscently. "It seems so odd to think that

I've only known you a little more than a month. To be honest, I can hardly believe that you are not truly my relation."

Touched, Amy returned her smile and remarked quietly that she believed that some females were born to be aunts. "Such useful creatures, you know."

Clarissa stared at her. "Surely you do not mean that you have given up all hope of marrying!"

"I am no longer in the first flush of youth," Amy pointed out. "And have worn a cap for many years."

"Pooh! What nonsense!" exclaimed the other. "To hear you talk one would think you in your dotage! As for your cap—only the other day Hugo was wondering why you wore it. You cannot be more than eight and twenty—which is not precisely ancient, you know. I daresay there are several gentlemen who would be only too pleased. . . . I've noticed that Mr. Fifield has a distinct liking for your company."

Amy, who had noticed the same thing, shook her head gently. "It would not do. I have no fortune and Mr. Fifield would not be a secretary if he had an income of his own, besides I do not—I have always hoped to marry someone I cared for—" She broke off, blushing a little, realizing suddenly that a totally unexpected and hitherto unperceived hope had risen in her heart sometime during the last few weeks.

"Aha! You care for someone," cried Clarissa with unexpected shrewdness. "You have a lover."

"Nothing of the kind," Amy told her quickly. "I am destined to be a maiden aunt, a useful spinster. And very well I shall do it."

"Poor Mr. Fifield," mourned Clarissa, apparently

accepting this. "How unhappy he would be if only he knew. Perhaps I can help him transfer his affections. . . . Withy, I am sure, would make an amiable wife. Would her little school make her acceptable, I wonder?"

"Wicked girl!" cried Amy. "You must do no such thing." She tried to speak severely, while inwardly she was amused by the thought of such an unlikely pairing, and attempted to turn Clarissa's attention to less contentious issues, but *The Lady's Journal* had lost all interest for her charge, who groaned with boredom.

"If only we could go out," she sighed. "I do not mean to make formal calls, but just to pay a visit to friends or go into the village, for I suppose Winchester to be too far for us to venture, without all the fuss of having to ask Tedbury to put the horses to and drive the coach. If only I could drive—how delightful it would be to take out Mama's little gig. It would be all the thing."

Amy looked up. "I can drive," she admitted.

Clarissa clapped her hands with joy. "Oh, admirable woman!" she cried, jumping to her feet and seizing Amy's hand. "We must go at once to the stables to look at the gig."

Nothing averse, Amy only stipulated that she would not take it out without Sir Hugo's permission, and both ladies spent a pleasant hour inspecting the various vehicles and petting the horses who inhabited the stables. The little black-and-yellow, round-ended gig was as well-kept as Clarissa remembered it, and so great was her enthusiasm for the proposed project that Amy was hard put to keep her from ordering Tedbury to put a horse between the shafts that very moment.

"Besides, he would, very rightly, *not* do so and only think how embarrassing that would be," she pointed out at last, and the girl finally gave in.

"Well, it will be the very first thing I ask Hugo," she promised. "I only hope he may return quickly for I am not at all patient, you know."

Sir Hugo was obliging enough to return within the week and, true to her word, Clarissa met him in the hall, demanding permission to use the gig.

"Only think how useful it would be, for in London it is quite the thing for ladies to drive unescorted in such a vehicle, so you need not be bothered at all," she pointed out ingenuously. "I daresay one of the stable boys could hitch up a horse in no time and Tedbury need have nothing to do with it at all. He is quite curmudgeonly lately. One would almost suppose the horses to be his."

Shrugging himself out of his driving coat, her brother regarded her with lazy amusement. "Your request would stand a better chance of success, Clary, if you allowed me a moment to refresh myself," he pointed out.

"I know that. I am not a complete ninny-head," she returned, taking his sleeve to coax him toward the study. "I have set out sherry and ratafia biscuits for you."

"Ratafias!" he exclaimed, revolted. "I prefer beer and cheese. I am not some maiden aunt, Sister."

"Don't eat them if you don't like them—but come and drink your sherry, which I am sure is more fashionable than beer, while I talk to you and *I'll* eat them, for there is nothing I like better and Mrs. Hill keeps close guard on them."

The outcome was that Amy was sent for and closely questioned upon her driving skills.

"My uncle taught me," she said with quiet composure.

Sir Hugo looked at her closely, a frown knitting his eyebrows. "Could that have been Flyer Standish, by any chance?" he wondered slowly.

Amy smiled. "We called him Uncle George," she returned. "He taught me some years ago, so I must confess to being a little rusty—but I believe that he was a notable horseman in his time."

"You could not have had a better teacher than George Standish. You may drive me out tomorrow, Cousin, to show me how well you handle the reins."

Knowing that she was on trial, Amy was somewhat nervous when she accompanied her employer to the stables next morning, but once seated in the gig, her fears vanished. Sir Hugo climbed in beside her and she was able to command the stable boy to stand aside with tolerable composure and even execute a little flourish of her whip as she caught the thong above her head, as she had been taught. Aware of the watchful eyes of Tedbury, she commanded the horse between the shafts to "walk on," and with a clatter of hooves, they trotted across the cobbled yard and came out onto the drive.

She was surprised when her companion directed her to drive away from the house, for she had supposed that she would be expected to show her abilities, or lack of them, on the estate paths before venturing farther.

"A student of Flyer Standish is not in need of mollycoddling," remarked a voice in her ear, and she knew that Sir Hugo had been aware of her supposition. "You shall drive me to the village. I know how my horse behaves in traffic—I intend to see how you manage under the same circumstances. We'll leave by the east gate."

Warned by the note in his voice, she was not surprised to discover that the proposed exit was a narrow affair settled between high stone pillars, approached by a twisting path, and closely lined by hedges so thick and tall that they gave the feeling of being enclosed in a passage.

She knew that she would have no second chance at negotiating the gateway and, setting the carriage up carefully, centered it nicely and was through without a scratch.

"Well done, Miss Standish," murmured the voice again. "We'll come back the same way to make sure it was not luck."

"Indeed, it was not!" she retorted, sparing him a speaking glance. "My uncle made me drive between two posts until I could judge it to an inch. To clip the paint would have been counted the greatest disgrace, I assure you."

The winding lane soon joined a wider road leading to Candover Magna and Amy recognized the church tower she could see from her window. Comfortable flint cottages lined the street, interspersed with a few larger houses. A black-and-white inn wearing a yellow thatch roof like a thick head of hair dominated the center of the village, facing across the green, now an expanse of damp grass, with a murky pond in the middle, but doubtless a meeting place for the local inhabitants in the summer when they could gather round the tall iron pump and share tidbits of gossip while drawing their water.

Amy noticed that children waved and the adults either bowed or curtsied as Sir Hugo passed, not in any obsequious manner, but rather as if happy to greet a respected friend, and she wondered anew at this man she and her mother supposed so hard and unkind. He seemed to know them all by name and Amy knew by the covert glances in her direction that her identity was a source of interest to them and remarked as much to her companion.

"Not a bit of it," he told her. "They will know all there is to know about you—probably more than I do!"

The startled glance she sent him was decidedly guilty, and meeting his bland gaze, she wondered if he had set a trap for her.

"Why, Cousin," Sir Hugo mused, "what can I have said to discompose you?"

"I am not used to country ways. You forget that I come from a city where privacy is valued."

"Of course," he answered readily, pausing before asking lightly: "And which city was that? I am sure I must know, but I appear to have forgotten."

Amy hesitated only fractionally before replying truthfully, "Portsmouth," having decided that the naval town was big enough to have housed both her sister and herself without exciting suspicion.

"Indeed—pray, turn here. We will skirt the green and then take the same road back to the Manor. Penn's mother also came from Portsmouth. You may have known her?"

"We lived very quietly," Amy replied constrainedly, concentrating on negotiating the space between a laden wagon and a farmer on a stout cob. "Portsmouth is very large, you know," she advised her companion kindly.

Apart from sending her a sharp glance, Sir Hugo let the matter drop and they continued in silence until they reached the east gate again and Amy was emboldened enough to flourish her whip as she drove through.

"Very pretty," was the dry comment as they bowled along the path. "As I had suspected when told of your tutor, you are a tolerable whip, Cousin, and I shall have no qualms about Clarissa driving out with you." As they arrived back at the stable yard and a boy ran to take the horse's head, he turned to her again to say quietly, "I know that I can rely upon your good sense to restrain the worst of her excesses. Her enthusiasms, as I am sure you are aware, can be both sudden and unacceptable. Clarissa tends to plunge through all opposition like a plough horse."

"You make her appear a wild, unrestrained girl and I must tell you that I have found her none of these things," Amy said, feeling called upon to defend her charge.

Sir Hugo smiled. "Cousin," he said softly, "you have not lived yet." And, having handed her down from the gig, he went on his way.

His sister's joy knew no bounds when Amy gave her news of Sir Hugo's approval, and she was full of plans for various expeditions at dinner that night.

"It will be very useful for you to be able to go to the village to collect your mail," observed Lucius.

Clarissa surveyed him with a frown. "What do you mean? I do not have many letters."

"Oh, come now, that cannot be true. You must be in hourly expectation of news from France." He looked from one blank face to the other. "I thought—forgive me if I am wrong, but I assumed after Lieutenant Masters's lengthy sojourn here the other day, when he was allowed to bid you farewell, that he must be accepted as a suitor and so, of course, allowed to correspond with you."

Clarissa looked thunderous, while Miss Standish's heart sank, but to her relief, Sir Hugo appeared to accept this interesting information with equanimity.

Scarcely looking up from cracking a nut, he said gently: "Ah, but then, my dear Lucius, due probably to the fact that you are a virtual newcomer to the family, you do not know that Kit Masters is a childhood friend of Clarissa's. It would have been a very odd thing if he had not bidden her farewell."

Clarissa beamed at her brother, who returned her look with his usual bland expression, while Lucius did his best not to appear aware of having just received one of his cousin's famous set-downs.

"Then we can expect to hear news of the war first-hand," he observed pleasantly. "I look forward, Clarissa, to daily bulletins from France. Indeed, you have probably been in receipt of a letter already. Do you have anything of interest to share with us?"

To her annoyance, Clarissa had to admit to not having heard from Kit, but pointed out carelessly that *she* was not at all surprised.

"Very wise," Sir Hugo put in. "Remember the weather, the distance, and the fluid nature of the campaign. We should not expect to hear until next week at the earliest."

Lucius gave a short laugh. "Remember, too, the youthful nature of the correspondent," he advised. "Master Masters will doubtless have more exciting matters to occupy him than to write to a childhood playmate!"

Not caring for the description, Clarissa glowered at him, unwilling to admit that she had taken to

130

watching for the arrival of the post in the hopes of being the recipient of a suitably devoted missive; as a languishing lover, Kit was proving somewhat unsatisfactory. "Did you never feel the call to arms, Lucius?" she asked pointedly. "I thought that perhaps you returned to England in order to join the army ... or the navy?"

Mr. Gambrill repressed a shudder. "I hope never to set foot on a ship again," he said devoutly. "As to buying a commission—of course I had hopes of serving my country. Indeed, it was my dearest wish, but ..." He shook his head sadly. "It was not to be."

"Why was that?" inquired Sir Hugo, interested.

"My health, you know. My constitution is not strong—we are all aware of the price we pay for living in the tropics." He gave a delicate cough, touching his handkerchief to his lips. "And my dear Mama, a devoted mother, knowing my intentions, extracted my promise not to even think of enlisting. I could not sail without arousing her anxiety. I am happy to say that we are a very united family."

Sir Hugo's eyes glinted with amusement, but he said nothing, and unable to think of any response to this evidence of filial duty, the other diners were silent until Mr. Fifield came to the rescue by inquiring politely if Miss Witherspoon had found the time to peruse the descriptions of the various properties he had given her.

"Indeed, indeed I have ... so very good of you, dear Mr. Fifield. I hardly know—all are so very nice and one *really* does not care to disappoint the hopeful owners. ..."

"You need have no fear of having to face them yourself. My man of business will manage it all

131

with perfect propriety, Miss Witherspoon," the baronet put in, understanding her difficulty. "No one will feel the least put out, I assure you."

The older woman looked relieved. "Oh, well, in that case, I feel that the house in May Square ... though, to be sure, the one on the high street is bigger. And then, of course, Magnificat Place has such an *uplifting* sound to it that I feel it would be perfect for a school ... *such* a moral tone for the pupils, you know." She looked round the table with haunted eyes. "I have gone over and over the papers," she confessed. "First one and then the other seems the most suitable. ... I know you will think me a foolish female, and perhaps I am, but— *Please*, Sir Hugo, tell me which to choose!"

"I think it would be best if Mr. Fifield took you on an inspection of all three tomorrow and gave you his advice," was his diplomatic reply. "Perhaps you, Cousin Almeria, and Clarissa, would care for a drive into Winchester?" he went on to suggest, with a hint of mischievousness that Amy was the only listener to suspect.

Lucius surprised them by declaring his willingness to accompany them, and so the next day the barouche was brought round to the front door and the three ladies and Mr. Gambrill settled themselves inside, while Sir Hugo's secretary accompanied them on one of the baronet's sturdy hunters.

Not altogether to Amy's surprise, Lucius Gambrill set himself out to amuse; not even Miss Witherspoon's flow of inanities served to ruffle his composure or bring forth a sharp rejoinder. As before, they left their transport at the Red Lion and set forth on foot to inspect the properties regarded as suitable to house Miss Witherspoon's school. The

132

high street proved to be, as was to be expected, a noisy thoroughfare. May Square was found to be too small, and by the time the party reached Magnificat Place, even though it was delightfully situated in the cathedral close, Clarissa could no longer conceal her boredom, sighing frequently and urging her ex-governess to make up her mind.

"I happened to notice a lending library in the high street," announced Lucius suddenly as they waited while Mr. Fifield found the key and ran up the steps to open the door. "If Clarissa would be so kind, I would value her aid in choosing a book. As we passed, I saw that they have received, just this morning, a parcel of new publications from London. One likes to keep up with the latest novels, you know."

Clarissa brightened and looked hopefully toward Amy, who nodded her agreement. "I believe we can manage without you," she teased. "Do not be late back at the inn. Tedbury has already remarked upon how much Sir Hugo dislikes the horses to be kept waiting."

Watching them walk away, Amy noticed that Lucius offered his arm with an unusual degree of gallantry and that he bent attentively over Clarissa as she accepted it. Amy's gaze grew speculative as she wondered if Sir Hugo's cousin was seeking an attachment to her charge; certainly Clarissa had been the recipient of more than usual attention lately and several times he had appeared to set himself out to please her. Consoling herself with the thought that Clarissa had a sensible head on her young shoulders and, being an heiress as well as a beauty, must be well used to being the object of flattery from men less wealthy than herself, Amy returned her attention to Miss Witherspoon and James Fifield who were discussing the points in favor of accepting Magnificat Place.

"Such a delightful setting—grass and trees just outside the door, almost like a garden. So suitable for the children ... I do think it so beneficial for little folk to have a daily walk, do not you agree, Miss Standish? And trees are so useful ... so leafy for shade in hot weather and just the thing for botany lessons and to teach the art of line drawing."

"We must look it over before you quite make up your mind," Mr. Fifield warned.

"To be sure—I am determined to be sensible, but must own to the most delightful feeling of having found precisely what I have always dreamed about."

The heavy black front door opened straight onto a large, sunny square hall, which Miss Witherspoon at once declared to be "so commodious, just the thing for receiving prospective parents." Two big rooms to either side were judged the right size for classrooms, and all in all, nothing could have made her change her mind as to the suitability of Magnificat Place, even if her two companions had so wished.

However, they both agreed with her, neither finding any difficulty in visualizing the house as a school, and having allowed her imagination free rein, they at last persuaded her to accompany them back to the inn to partake of refreshments before setting off on the return journey.

Mr. Fifield left the ladies drinking China tea and eating slices of rich fruitcake, while he and the vendor's lawyers undertook the serious business of agreeing on the clauses in the renting contract.

Soon Clarissa and Lucius Gambrill put in an appearance and Amy could not help but notice that her charge's eyes were bright and that they both had the air of finding pleasure in each other's company.

"Did you find a book you liked?" she asked, pouring tea.

"Oh, no," murmured Clarissa absently as she accepted the cup from her cousin. "We went for a walk instead. And I must own the truth that I have not enjoyed anything so much for a long time. Such sights we saw. *So* many ancient females in such quizzes of hats as to make one die laughing! I can tell you, Aunt Almeria, that I was hard put to hide my mirth. The ogling, flirtations, and assignations between the rustic maidens, decked in their finery, and the bold soldiery on leave from the local barracks, I declare, was as good as a play!"

"I daresay that they had no intention of providing amusement," Amy said in reproof, "and would have felt embarrassment if they had known that they were doing so."

Clarissa had the grace to blush. "No need to be a sobersides; I assure you, we were discretion itself. . . . We met little Jemmie Peel outside his father's shop. He gave me the quaintest bow and sent you a kiss—I received mine in person. Lucius was quite taken with him. I don't know how many times he heard the tale of Master Jemmie's abduction and rescue!"

Amy looked at the gentleman, pensively munching fruitcake. "I would not have supposed you to have felt interest in a sticky butcher's child," she remarked.

135

Roused out of his reverie, he stared blankly at her for a few seconds before, summoning up a smile, he said: "To be honest, I was amazed at the resilience displayed by the lower classes. If one of *our* children had been taken, we would never allow them out alone again, and yet here was Master Jemmie, as bold as nine-pence, free to roam the streets in the hope that he had learned to be wiser." He gave a shudder. "Let us hope that the would-be abductor has left the vicinity—one does not feel safe with a criminal gang of child-thieves on the rampage!"

CHAPTER EIGHT

With the better weather, Mr. Gambrill found the need to visit his tailor in London and the ladies were thrown back on their own resources for amusement, for which Amy was rather grateful, feeling, as she did, that Lucius's attentions toward Clarissa were growing altogether too marked. Somewhat to her surprise, Sir Hugo appeared indifferent to the situation, watching with lazy amusement whenever he happened to be made aware of it. If she had a choice, Amy thought, as to a suitor for Clarissa's hand, she would prefer Sir Simon Lovell, and when her charge suggested, on a particularly springlike day, that they should drive over to view the drifts of snowdrops for which Peninsula House was well-known, she agreed readily.

Clarissa looked especially charming in sky blue velvet, while the bright weather inspired Miss Standish to wear a newly acquired amber-colored pelisse and bonnet trimmed with matching amber ribbons. Pleasantly conscious that they were looking their best, they bowled along the lanes whose hedges were showing the merest hint of green, the pony drawing the gig seeming as happy as they were to feel the first warmth of the year.

"Should we call on Sir Simon?" Amy suggested casually.

"To be sure, we can see the flowers from the road but it would be churlish to pass by, would it not?" was her charge's considered reply.

"Almost impolite," agreed Amy and finding themselves in complete accord, they exchanged smiles.

Peninsula House was built on a rise above the road, a small Palladian building, rather low and elegant, with long windows and a porticoed entrance. The spring sunshine made its white stucco gleam brightly and the lawns that fell away in a graceful sweep were almost covered by snowdrops, thick enough to resemble a green-and-white carpet.

"Oh, how pretty!" Amy exclaimed, drawing on the reins as she gazed upward in admiration. "Usually, you know, I do not particularly care for modern houses, but this is—perfect."

"Yes," agreed her companion. "It's certainly very convenient . . . and I do like the snowdrops."

Amy laughed at her. "Philistine!" she teased and clicked her tongue to make the horse walk on.

He slowed a little on the climb upward, but picked up speed when they reached flat ground and they arrived in front of the house at a spanking pace, his hooves striking smartly and the accoutrements jingling cheerfully.

As they reached the front door, it was opened and Lieutenant Lovell ran down the steps to meet them.

"My dear Miss Dysart—and Miss Standish! How delightful to see you," he said. "If only I could be sure it was myself whom you have called to see, I should be entirely happy, but to be truthful, I have

138

already received two visitors today who made no bones about wishing to view my snowdrops!"

"In all honesty, it was indeed the snowdrops that brought us—but only a *friend's* flowers could be called upon, I imagine," observed Amy, accepting his hand as she descended the short step down from the vehicle.

"Just so," he agreed gravely, before allowing his gaze to dwell in appreciation upon Clarissa's laughing face. "Of course, they are old friends to you," he remarked, reluctant to release her hand although she had safely reached the ground.

"I must own that I am glad that you live here," she told him. "Only think if some curmudgeonly, disagreeable person had charge of my former home and I could only glimpse it from the road." Looking round, she sighed with satisfaction. "I must say that for a City merchant, my grandpapa had extraordinary good taste. He built this, you know, and my mama was married from here."

"Will you take refreshments? My housekeeper is, this very minute, pouring water into the teapot and setting out cakes and biscuits. She will be disappointed if you refuse her offering—we can view the garden later."

The ladies were agreeable to this and the lieutenant escorted them indoors to a room furnished in the Japanese style: all light wallpaper, delicate, elegant furniture, and the bright, clear colors usually found on Japanese porcelain.

As she settled herself beside the fire, Amy thought that she preferred the worn homeliness of Candover Magna, but Clarissa appeared happy in her surroundings, accepting the position of tea-pourer with equanimity. Watching, Amy was

139

pleased to see that Clarissa's former embarrassment seemed to have worn off and that she treated Sir Simon with easy friendliness. Briefly she wondered if the girl was aware of the regard in which the lieutenant held her, which to an informed observer was obvious, but decided that Clarissa was so used to being the center of attention, so sure of her consequence, that she thought such care to her comfort nothing more than due to her. She sighed a little with unconscious regret for something she had never had and Lieutenant Lovell looked up quickly.

"Forgive me. I am neglecting you," he said quietly, coming to her side. "Is something bothering you? I could not help hearing you sigh."

She shook her head, looking across the room to Clarissa's bright head. "Just passing envy," she confessed with a rueful smile. "To be the possessor of both wealth and beauty can only be considered excessive by lesser females."

"I know you are funning—but do not decry yourself even in play, Miss Standish," he reproved. "You are the possessor of an elegance that many strive after and that money cannot provide."

With the impetuosity of youth, Clarissa chose that moment to jump to her feet and declare herself impatient to renew her acquaintance with the garden, and Amy was saved from having to reply to the lieutenant's unexpected compliment.

Clarissa's grandfather had had a lifelong interest in gardening that, when he retired from the City, verged upon the obsessive. He had supervised every stage of the gardens, from laying out the various banks and beds to planting trees, with the enthusiasm of an amateur Capability Brown. Finding a spring above the house, he had caused a stream to be cut and a series of rocky waterfalls contrived to tumble, in the most natural manner, into a small pond below the house.

"Have you inherited his interest, Miss Clarissa?" asked Sir Simon, as they admired the effect.

Clarissa shook her head. "I like it, of course, but must own to finding gardening a lengthy business. Have you never noticed how *long* everything takes? By the time a plant has flowered, I would have forgotten what it was! My cousin, Lucius, says I would like the tropics, where things grow and flower almost overnight."

"Is Mr. Gambrill interested in horticulture?"

Clarissa could not resist a gurgle of laughter at the unlikely thought. "I do not believe that Lucius would recognize a spade if he saw one. Indeed, I do not know what interests him—save social life and fashion. At the moment he is combining the two and spending a few days in London."

Sir Simon frowned. "But surely I saw him in Winchester only yesterday?"

"Oh, no. He left for Town the day before, eager to have a new coat cut and to meet up with his cronies. Besides, he has told me that he regards Winchester as a dead bore, so I am certain he would not slip away to spend time there."

Still looking unconvinced, Sir Simon shrugged his shoulders. "I daresay I was mistaken—to be honest, the man I saw appeared to be speaking to a ruffian very like the one Miss Standish dealt with, which, if it had been your cousin, would have been even more puzzling."

"That cannot have been Lucius," Clarissa stated positively. "He would never have anything to do with such a person. Why, he even avoids noticing that the servants exist! I am afraid that he is not at all democratic!"

"I daresay it comes from living in the West Indies," observed Amy. "It cannot be good for one's character to be a slave owner."

Clarissa looked up quickly. "*Surely* Lucius does not keep slaves!" she cried.

"Almost certainly, I'd say," Amy returned. "However much you may disagree with the practice, I believe the wealth of the sugar plantations is founded upon slave labor."

The younger girl looked horror-stricken but unconvinced and Amy turned to their companion, who had been quietly listening to this exchange. "What do you think, Sir Simon?"

"I agree with you. The whole economy is based on slaves working in the cane fields and factories. I have intercepted a slave ship, myself, Miss Clarissa, an experience I have no wish to repeat and one that I would not care to relate to you. Let it be said that I support Mr. Wilberforce in his efforts to abolish the abominable trade in human beings."

Clarissa stared at him, her comfortable world disturbed by his bald words. For a moment, Amy thought that she would demand to know more, but then the girl looked away, obviously preferring to remain in ignorance of the horrors beyond her secure existence. Disappointed, for she had hopes that her charge might have intelligence and compassion enough to see beyond her own frivolous life, Amy followed as the naval officer led Clarissa on a tour of the grounds.

"Do you know, Aunt Almeria, I found our visit

quite enjoyable. Why, I do not know, for after all, Peninsula House and its grounds are nothing new to me," Clarissa remarked on the way home.

"Sir Simon makes a good host," the older woman answered, with a sidelong glance at her charge.

The girl considered this. "Certainly one feels comfortable with him. There is no need to be always minding one's manners or taking care to be witty and charming."

Her day was made when, arriving home, she found a letter from Kit on the hall table. With a cry of joy, she seized it and ran upstairs to read it in the privacy of her room. News of the letter had gone round the household and when the inmates of the Manor gathered for dinner that night, with Clarissa obviously bursting with suppressed excitement, it was not long before the fact was casually brought into conversation in the expectation of learning the contents.

"Of all things marvelous! Kit is on his way home!" she announced, eager to share her information. "My dearest Kit writes that he hopes to be at Carley Weston next week."

Sir Hugo looked at her keenly. "How so?" he demanded. "Something untoward would be the only thing to earn him leave of absence with the threat of the army about to see action."

"Kit's scrawl was ever difficult to decipher and this was writ in great hurry—he says he had a great adventure on the way to join his regiment and was the means of rescuing a little girl called Marie Savy, whom he has been given leave to escort home to his mother, whom he is sure will take her under her wing."

The diners round the table gazed at her in aston-

143

ishment. "A child? Of what age?" queried Mr. Fifield.

"Oh, quite small, I imagine. He writes that she is the 'sweetest little thing,'" replied Clarissa airily. "And that we are all sure to love her and that she will be a sister for Sarah."

Sir Hugo's eyebrows shot up. "I had not supposed Kit to be particularly enamored of children," he remarked.

"I daresay I am being foolish, but, really, one cannot help wondering—why would he bring a little French child here?" asked Miss Witherspoon. "Surely it would be best to leave her with her parents—"

"Children can become separated from their family if they happen to be caught up in a skirmish," the baronet supplied, "but even so, it seems somewhat odd that Kit should involve himself and that his commander should encourage him."

"Poor little thing! Only think how unhappy she must be. I shall look out my old toys for her, this very day. What a good thing I found them only recently in the attic. I may even give her Arabella Melancholy—" She paused to consider this piece of generosity, adding quickly, after a moment's reflection, that as the doll was rather shabby and old-fashioned, it might be a better idea to purchase and dress a new one.

"Perhaps it would be wiser to wait and see how old she is," suggested Miss Standish quietly, but Clarissa pooh-poohed the idea, declaring her certainty that the girl was a mere toddler, and Miss Witherspoon immediately set about imagining the difficulties of integrating a French child into her proposed school.

144

"Of course, even *good* children can be a little unkind—not that I would allow . . . but *French*, and we *are* at war. With a name like Marie Savy—so very foreign sounding, you know, there could be no possible hope of hiding her nationality."

"We must all take Cousin Almeria's wise council and wait to see," put in Sir Hugo with finality, growing tired of the speculation.

Finding herself quite unable to imagine Lieutenant Masters playing nursemaid to a small girl, a thought had occurred to Amy, but as no one else appeared to share it and Clarissa was obdurate that the refugee could not be other than barely out of napkins, she kept her unfounded suspicions to herself.

Mr. Gambrill returned before the end of the week and was at once regaled with the story. He appeared quite unimpressed with the young man's philanthropy, stating his belief that such a gesture showed a sad lack of patriotism. At this blow to her hero, Clarissa became quite irritable and told him soundly that if anyone was in want of anything, it was himself who stood in need of both generosity and sensibility. Realizing that he had made a mistake, Lucius Gambrill at once declared that he had misunderstood the matter and that nothing could be more noble than to care for the child of one's enemy, upon which good relations were restored and he was allowed to give advice upon the respective merits of pink or blue for a doll's dress.

Mr. Gambrill had brought the latest news of the British advance across France with him from London and, once Clarissa's on-dit had been dealt with, the gentlemen returned as quickly as good manners allowed to the more important matters of the

145

war and the shocking information that the general himself had been wounded.

"It will take more than a spent bullet to disable the field marshal," Sir Hugo stated with authority. "The man's as tough as a Mogul and as fly as one of his own riflemen. Mere bruising will be brushed off as of no account."

"I feel that he takes too many risks," put in Mr. Fifield judiciously. "The army has need of him—spies and guides can be found among the rank and file. Not so a field marshal."

A reminiscent smile hovered over his patron's mouth. "He was ever one to do his own reconnoitering. He likes to see the lay of the land for himself."

"Indeed—but in a man of importance and standing, sense should prevail," Mr. Gambrill stated ponderously.

"It should be a short affair now—with the rivers crossed and Marshal Soult driven out of Orthez, it can only be a matter of weeks before Paris falls. Pray Heaven that Foreign Secretary Castlereagh achieves a peace settlement from his meeting with our allies and the French general, Caulaincourt, at Chatillon. It's high time this business was ended."

"I cannot imagine not being at war," Clarissa suddenly remarked. "We have been fighting the French since I was a little girl. How strange it will be to be at peace. Will the army be demobbed? How I shall miss seeing the men in the glory of their regimentals!"

"Have no fear, Clary. There is still America to be dealt with," was her brother's dry reply.

"But America is so far away!" his sister protested, allowing the hint of a pout to appear.

"Then you will just have to turn your attention

146

to men in drab, civilian clothes and forget your scarlet-coated popinjays!" retorted Sir Hugo. "We cannot be kept in a state of war merely to satisfy your liking for uniforms!"

"Clarissa has my sympathy," put in Amy. "I must confess to having lost my heart many times to a dashing hero in red, only to find that shorn of his uniform and without his accoutrements and swagger, he proved to be a very poor fellow."

Sir Hugo lifted his lazy gaze. "Is that so, Cousin?" he drawled. "I had not suspected you of being so fickle. Let me remind you that I was once a soldier and do not, by any means, consider myself a poor fellow."

Miss Standish lowered her eyes. "Ah, but then, no one could say that *you* have lost your swagger!" she murmured.

Reaching along the table, his long fingers closed over her wrist as she held the stem of her wineglass. "Flirting, Miss Standish?" he asked, for her ears alone.

Startled by his plain speaking, her eyes flew to his face and what she saw there made her catch her breath. "I—am sadly out of practice," she admitted and he held her a moment longer, letting her feel his strength.

"I am quite willing to be practiced upon," he said, releasing her wrist.

No one appeared to have noticed the little incident and, as her heartbeat returned to normal, Amy became aware that the conversation had continued around the table, and that, now the weather had improved, the diners were discussing the possibility of arranging an expedition to the nearby ruins of a Norman castle.

Clarissa turned sparkling eyes upon her brother. "Oh, Hugo, do say we may!" she cried. "An adventure would be just the thing, for life has been so *dull* lately. I vow we all could benefit from a little excitement."

Sir Hugo agreed readily, surprising them all by declaring himself willing to make up one of the party. Clarissa made no effort to curb her impatience and, quite carried away with the prospect, urged that the excursion should take place the very next day, weather permitting.

To her undisguised delight, the morning dawned bright and clear, with promise of a perfect spring day. Mindful of the probable mud underfoot, the ladies donned their winter boots, which had been left off at the first hint of spring, and firmly buttoned into woolen pelisses and carrying shawls, took their places in the barouche with a lively, excited Penn, who had been let off lessons as a special treat, between them. Clarissa had proposed the use of the landaulet, but Sir Hugo had vetoed the idea, pointing out that an open coach would not be prudent so early in the year.

"We can let the top down if we should be hot," she said to comfort herself as they set off.

Lucius shared the coach, while Sir Hugo and his secretary rode beside. By a happy thought on Sir Hugo's part, an invitation to Sir Simon had been sent, and as they passed Peninsula House, the lieutenant rode out to join them.

Leaning forward, Clarissa waved her gloved hand, remarking thoughtfully that a naval uniform was nearly as becoming as a military one.

Mr. Gambrill expressed his opinion that a well-fitting, superfine civilian coat was as smart as ei-

ther and, upon no one agreeing with him, retired
into huffy silence for some minutes, until brought
out of his sulk by Penn, who had been inspecting
him for some time, remarking upon the pretty color
of the pantaloons he was sporting.

"Just like the paint in the kitchen," he observed.

Since the paint in question was a particularly
virulent shade of mustard, which everyone agreed
had been a mistake, no one replied to this interesting comment. Lucius Gambrill, who thought his leg
covers a fashionable canary yellow, compressed his
lips, endeavoring to subdue the boy with a glare,
but Penn returned his gaze innocently.

"*Just* like," he repeated with satisfaction. "Don't
kick me, Clary—it's a very *nice* color—like . . . like
the mustard pickles Mrs. Hill makes!"

"Tell me about Castle Malreward, Clarissa," Amy
put in hastily as Lucius's complexion reddened
alarmingly. "Such an unusual name, I am sure,
must have a tale behind it."

Doing her best to stifle her giggles, Clarissa
obeyed. "One of the Henrys gave it to a knight,
William D'Eath, who was less than pleased with
his reward and, not being one to hide his feelings,
named it so."

"He must have been either brave or foolhardy to
risk offending the King," mused Amy, and was considerably relieved when the coach breasted a hill at
that moment and the object of their outing came
into view, distracting Penn from the subject of Mr.
Gambrill's pantaloons.

From a distance, the castle looked in remarkably
good condition, but as Tedbury drove nearer, it became clear that only the foursquare keep was in a
state of some preservation. Despite its empty door

149

and gaping black windows, it still presented an impregnable air, standing grim and resolute on its knoll, surrounded by a grassy ditch that at one time had been its moat.

Eyeing it with interest, Penn hung out of the barouche the better to see. "Can I go up to the top?" he asked, dangling out so perilously that Amy grabbed the seat of his nankeen trousers. "I want to see where the soldiers were."

"You must ask Sir Hugo," she told him. "Ruins can be dangerous places."

"I'm brave," he assured her as the coach came to a halt and Sir Hugo opened the door. Unfortunately Penn was at once struck by a previous thought and surveyed his uncle's restrained green cutaway coat and pale cream buckskin breeches with a disparaging gaze. "Why don't you have pickle-trousers, too?" he demanded.

Sir Hugo did not pretend ignorance. "Because, brat, I do not aspire to be a sprig of fashion," Penn was told as he was lifted out and deposited on the ground. "I see you have an admirer, Lucius," Sir Hugo remarked easily as he handed out the ladies.

"They are all the go in Town," his cousin assured him defensively.

Sir Hugo allowed his gaze to wander over the other man. "I daresay," he agreed. "And such a pretty color, too. Penn has a remarkable power of description for his age."

Mr. Gambrill looked about to give one of his sharp replies but, meeting Sir Hugo's eyes, merely remarked lightly upon his funning nature and, offering Clarissa his arm, was first to head up the path to the castle.

The company spent a pleasant hour or so exploring the ruins and their surroundings. The narrow twisting staircase built in the wall of the keep was entire, if somewhat perilous, and they were able to climb to the battlements and walk around the walls where sentries had patrolled centuries before. Penn was enthralled by the thought and took to marching around in a very military way. From their vantage point, Peninsula House could be clearly identified by its white walls, while beyond, the twisting chimneys and lazy blue smoke of Candover Magna rose above the trees that surrounded it.

Descending again, they found that Tedbury had deposited the hamper and a rug and retired to a distance with the carriage, where he could be seen consuming his own lunch, with the horses tethered nearby. Mr. Fifield took it upon himself to show off his expertise in lighting a fire to boil the kettle, and soon the ladies were anticipating a cup of tea while enjoying the delights of the alfresco meal supplied by Mrs. Hill.

"One wonders why we are expected to feel sorry for the lower classes," mused Clarissa, daintily licking her fingers as her companions warily waited for her to enlighten them. "I declare that nothing can be nicer than eating a chicken wing with one's fingers!"

"I don't suppose that they would complain if they had chicken to eat—I believe it is the fact of their not having enough to eat that arouses sympathy," pointed out Mr. Fifield studiously.

"Well, eating in the fresh air, as I believe they often do, must give them a good appetite. I daresay I would eat like a horse, too, if I took my meals outside!"

"Do not be more of a pea-goose than you can

151

help, Clarissa," put in her brother, lying at her feet with his hands clasped behind his head. "I am persuaded that even you must know that many poor people do not have enough to eat."

"Oh—well, of *course* I am aware of that! I just thought that if they were not so much out of doors, they would not be so hungry," she explained, ingenuously.

Sir Hugo opened his gray eyes and she flushed under his quelling look. "Sometimes I wonder what you learned during all the years I have paid for your education," he remarked coldly.

"Oh, dear ... I did not realize that you wished—I do not believe that we studied the working classes," twittered Miss Witherspoon in obvious distress. "I did not know that you required—indeed, I am afraid that I am not qualified—though to be sure, I do not precisely know how to find out—"

"Do not worry, Miss Witherspoon," he interrupted, sitting up abruptly. "Penury was not one of the required subjects in Clarissa's curriculum! I merely supposed that someone of normal intellect would have come by some knowledge of how the other half of the kingdom lives."

Amy felt called upon to defend her charge. "As far as I can see, Sir Hugo, Clarissa has lived the sheltered life expected of an upper-class female. How could she be expected to have learned of the hardship and deprivation suffered by the underprivileged?"

Gray eyes frowned at her. "I am fairly certain that *you* have an understanding of their problems—"

"I am not upper class," she reminded him.

"I will have you know that I am no more chuckle-headed than the next person," put in Clarissa crossly. "Let me tell you, Brother, that you are able to mix with common folk at mills and—and horse races. Where am I supposed to meet them? Next time I see a suitably poor person, I shall ask Tedbury to stop so that I may ask them a few questions!"

Sir Hugo's expression darkened, but at that opportune moment Sir Simon wondered upon the whereabouts of Penn and the threatening quarrel was nipped in the bud as the opponents and the rest of the party looked around in search of the small boy.

A few hearty "halloos" having elicited no response, and the surroundings being empty of any sign of a small figure, the group separated, going different ways, and Amy soon found herself alone at the overgrown base of the towering keep. Scrubby undergrowth provided a perfect playground for a child and she spent some time calling and pushing aside tangled grass and trailing bushes, until a movement high up on the farthest corner of the tower attracted her attention. Looking up, she saw a familiar figure, standing on top of a crenellation, in the act of hurling something to the ground sixty feet below.

Her first instinct was to cry out, but realizing the danger of startling Penn, she smothered her call and backed away, as if by keeping her eyes fastened on him, he would not fall. Rounding the corner she came upon Sir Hugo who had also realized the delights, for a small, adventurous boy, of the tangled undergrowth, and running up to him, she made known her discovery.

153

Turning on his heels, the baronet plunged into the gaping doorway behind him and she could hear the echo of his pounding footsteps as he hurled himself up the spiral staircase. Almost against her will, she returned to where she had seen Penn creeping along the stone wall, in dread at what she might find. No small boy lay crumpled on the stony ground and she raised her eyes, as another stone landed on the grass at her feet, to see him still engaged in his game on the battlements.

Leaning against the wall, one hand pressed to her racing heart, she held her breath, willing the child not to fall. As she watched anxiously, a figure came into view, whom she at first took to be Sir Hugo. As it silently crept toward the boy, a flash of mustard yellow identified the man as Lucius, his hand, palm outward, stretched toward the unconscious child, and instead of relief a totally unexpected fear shot through Amy. As she took an involuntary step forward, the hand turned, the fingers hooked into Penn's jacket, and the boy was jerked out of danger. At the same moment Sir Hugo appeared beside Lucius to snatch his nephew into the safety of his arms and for a moment all three were silhouetted against the bright spring sky like a tableau from a play.

A grim-faced Sir Hugo handed a howling Penn to Amy as she ran to meet them at the foot of the stairs. "You deserve a whipping," he told his nephew, looking ready to administer it there and then.

"The fright he has had will deter him from doing it again," Amy said, as the boy hid his face against her shoulder.

"He has no idea of the danger—the odious brat is

154

crying because his game was disturbed," Sir Hugo commented in exasperated tones.

"I—I'm—a *soldier*!" roared Penn, confirming his uncle's views. "You're a bad man—I don't *like* you!"

"Hush, darling," Amy said soothingly. "We know you were having an exciting game, but it is dangerous up there. You might have fallen and hurt yourself very badly." She buried her face in his dark curls at the thought of what might have happened.

"He should be beaten," said Lucius, arriving in the doorway behind them. "Disobedient children should be punished. I was never allowed to behave so."

Sir Hugo looked at his cousin, abruptly shifting his ground and reversing his previous view. "Penn has had fright enough," he said in a voice that brooked no argument. "Besides, I fancy that he was in more danger from you than from himself—"

Mr. Gambrill's face whitened. "What do you mean? I saved the boy. You saw me yourself."

There was a long pause, while Sir Hugo studied his cousin. "I saw that you were in danger of startling him," he said at last, turning away to take the now hiccupping Penn from Amy and set him on his feet. "Now, brat, you and I have a few things to discuss," he said quietly, taking his hand to lead him away across the grass.

Clarissa turned pale and had to be supported by Sir Simon's ready arm when Mr. Gambrill regaled her with the adventure and his own part in it.

"Do not be so feeble, Clarissa," Sir Hugo advised with evident disgust. "Cousin Almeria, who saw the whole thing, has found no cause to swoon!"

"Miss Dysart is a female of much sensibility," put in the lieutenant as she drooped against his blue uniform. "I must admit that I find such delicacy admirable."

"If you'd known her as long as I have, you would grow a little tired of regular histrionics at every opportunity," retorted her brother, whose eyes lingered as if by chance on Miss Standish as he added: "I appreciate a female who keeps her head and remains calm and useful!"

CHAPTER NINE

The excitements of the day were not over, for upon returning to the Manor, it was discovered that Mrs. Masters had sent a note over with the news that Kit had arrived home and that she hoped to have the honor of presenting Mademoiselle Marie Savy to them and would take the liberty of calling upon them on the next day.

"Of all things delightful!" enthused Clarissa, clasping the note to her bosom and executing a very lively waltz around the hallway. "To see my dearest Kit and have the pleasure of knowing dear little Marie who, I am convinced, must be the sweetest child imaginable. She will make the best of playmates for Penn, who will be a brother to her!"

Amy looked at her doubtfully. "I fear you run ahead of yourself," she said. "The child might well be older than we believe—may be much older—possibly too old to play with Penn."

"Pooh, what nonsense! Kit calls her the 'sweetest little thing' and you must know that *that* is not at all the way he would describe a roisterous half-grown girl!"

Amy had to concede the truth of this but, still feeling a vague uneasiness, felt the need to curb the worst of her charge's enthusiasm, pointing out how foolish she would feel if the planned welcome should prove totally unsuitable. "For French infants are much more sophisticated than ours," she warned.

How wise she had been became clear the next day; the ladies were seated over their sewing in the parlor when the sound of heavy wheels trundling purposefully toward the front door made them all look up.

"My dearest Kit!" exclaimed Clarissa, dropping the handkerchief she had been hemming and flying to the window where she exclaimed abruptly and clutched wildly at the curtain.

The harsh ejaculation brought Amy to her side, puzzled by the girl's rigid stance. With a steadying hand on her shoulder, she followed her wildly staring gaze to the coach below and saw the familiar figure in a scarlet uniform in the act of handing the diminutive form of a very fashionably dressed young lady to the ground. A laughing face peeped out from the deep brim of a fetching royal blue poke bonnet. A riot of black curls framed a delightfully roguish pair of dark eyes and a pair of tiny, expensive kid boots showed momentarily as their owner tripped lightly toward the house, leaning possessively on Lieutenant Masters's willing arm.

"Oh—*dear!*" Amy murmured on seeing the confirmation of her wildest suspicions, and closed her eyes to shut out the unwelcome sight. Opening them again, she found that Clarissa was still standing transfixed, her fingers white where she gripped the velvet folds. "Clarissa—Clarissa!" she cried, seizing her by the shoulders to shake her unresponsive form. "You must pull yourself together—" Blue eyes stared blankly at her. "Clary, wake up!" she urged and was relieved to see intelligence return to the stunned gaze. "You must go down to greet them," she told the girl.

Clarissa's eyes flickered. "Never!" she cried, her breast heaving. "Never! The hussy—to hang on Kit's arm in that way." Her face crumpled. "How *could* he?" she wailed. "To bring her here—when I thought that we—"

Gathering her close, Amy hugged her shivering body. "Oh, Clary, my love. I think there has been a misunderstanding!" And, looking back, she could see that it might well be so. "But now you must control your feelings and go down to meet them."

"No!" Clarissa shook her head violently.

"My dear girl, you must. Don't you see it's the only thing to do, if you do not wish to be the object of speculation?" Amy pointed out relentlessly. "You must pretend so well as to convince everyone that all you ever felt for Kit was sisterly friendship. You do not want to be an object of sympathy among your friends and the local society, do you? If you act the part of a friend, you may carry it off without comment. Refuse to meet Kit and Mademoiselle Savy, and you will be the center of rumor and gossip. Only think how amused society will be, and there will not be a dearth of other, less beautiful females only too willing to laugh behind their fans at the downfall of an attractive heiress!"

"Oh, Aunt Almeria—I thought . . . I truly believed that we l-loved each other."

She looked and sounded so desolate that Amy would have given much for a moment alone with Lieutenant Masters in which to enlighten that young man upon a few matters. Instead, she wiped

159

the tears from Clarissa's cheeks and brushed back her curls, looking deeply into her charge's eyes. "Be brave," she urged.

Clarissa summoned up a tremulous smile. "I will," she promised sadly. "No one will ever guess that my heart is broken."

And gathering together her damaged dignity, she crossed to the door with the air of a tragedy queen. She paused on the way to express her emotions by picking up the newly dressed doll, dropping it contemptuously on the floor, and kicking it viciously across the room. Dusting her fingers, she sailed on, her head high, and Amy followed, feeling a rush of proud affection.

"Mrs. Masters, how delightful to see you," Clarissa called as she descended the stairs. Reaching the bottom, she gave Kit her hand for a brief moment, before turning to smile at the tiny figure brought forward by his mother.

"Clarissa, my dear, let me present Mademoiselle Marie Savy," Mrs. Masters said. "Marie, this is Kit's dearest friend, of whom I have told you."

"Mademoiselle." Clarissa inclined her head graciously. "I long to hear your adventures, but first let me introduce my aunt, Miss Almeria Standish, and Miss Witherspoon, my companion."

Amy bowed and said a few pleasant words before asking an interested Mrs. Hill to arrange for the tea tray to be brought into the withdrawing room, but Mary Witherspoon, who had been a bemused spectator of the incident upstairs and who had followed them down to the hall in a state of bewilderment, gazed in a puzzled fashion at the entrancing figure in dark blue silk spencer and clinging, white muslin and inquired plaintively as to the whereabouts of the little French child she expected to see.

"Miss Witherspoon, what a tease you are," chided Amy gently. "Only pray remember that Kit will not be aware of what you mean." Turning to the young man, she explained: "From your letter we were a little uncertain of the age of your protégée, and Miss Witherspoon supposed she might even be of an age to fill a place in her school!"

They all laughed and Mary Witherspoon, supposing herself to have said something witty, joined in happily.

Kit Masters behaved impeccably, handing round cups and plates and waiting on the ladies with all the gallantry and charm of a much older man, but no one could mistake the doting glances he bestowed on the French girl when he thought himself unobserved, or the confiding way she turned to him when she did not understand, or the ready way he translated.

Amy found herself seated beside Mrs. Masters and noticed that lady's thoughtful gaze on her son as Kit bent attentively over the lively girl, who was laughing up into his face. Turning her head, the older woman became aware that Amy's eyes, too, dwelt upon the handsome couple, and leaning a little closer, she confided quietly:

"I thought it best that we visit here first. I do so hope that Kit was right. He assures me that there never was more than friendship between himself and Clarissa ... but to be honest, I have thought lately that her feelings were warmer. I have been so worried that the poor child will be hurt, for I am afraid there is no concealing my foolish son's infatuation with Marie."

Amy was at a loss about what to reply, quickly deciding that played-down truth was the best answer. "There can be no doubt that Clarissa is very fond of Kit and, to all who know her, made no attempt to hide her romantic dreams. . . . She is, after all, very young. But she is a sensible child whose pride will not let the affair become common gossip. With care, I am sure we can carry the matter off with no one the wiser."

"Poor child! Oh, I do so hope so. The blighting effect of an early rejection can have far-reaching consequences and I would not have her youthful hopes shattered."

"I believe that Clarissa is made of sterner stuff," Amy assured her, hoping that she spoke the truth. "We must work together to pass it off lightly and make sure that no one has cause for speculation or rumor."

Across the room, Clarissa gave a tinkling laugh that, only to Miss Standish's attuned ears, carried a hint of strained nerves. Looking up, Clarissa caught her eye and called a trifle desperately for her to join them.

"Aunt Almeria, you must hear the story of Kit's adventure. It is the most exciting thing. Only think, he found Madamoiselle Marie about to be carried off by a group of Cuirassiers—they are heavily armored cavalry, you know. Her mama is English and having found this out, they supposed her to be a spy."

"She hardly needed my help, Miss Standish, for she was sitting her horse like a regular hussar, belaboring the Frenchies with her riding crop. They were so demoralized that it only took one hurrah and a charge from me, to make them turn tail and

162

flee—of course, they thought I had a regiment at my heel," he added modestly.

"No—no, it was not so!" cried Marie Savy, clasping his hand fondly. " 'E was ze 'ero! So brave in coming to my rescue—I can never forget it."

Her accent was as delightful as her appearance and Lucius Gambrill, who had entered unseen, could only stand and gaze in astonishment at this entrancing creature, appearing in her bright plumage rather like a tiny exotic bird amid a group of drab English sparrows.

A discreet cough drew their attention and he was brought forward to be introduced. Amy saw his brows contract at the name and his eyes flew toward Clarissa, but he hid any surprise he felt at the age of Kit's protégée and blandly complimented both rescuer and rescued.

With the ease of long acquaintance, the party stayed longer than the regulation quarter of an hour, but Mrs. Masters did not allow the visit to linger, and soon gathered them to her and took her departure.

"How very odd to be sure," began Mr. Gambrill, as their coach could be heard driving away. "I must own to some surprise at the age of Master Masters's 'sweetest little thing.' " He turned a speculative gaze on his cousin. "Allow me to compliment you, Clarissa, on the way in which you hid your own surprise. Under the circumstances, it was the only thing to be done."

Clarissa glared at him. "What a man for compliments—three in the space of as many minutes!" she remarked acidly. "As for Kit Masters—I own to having grown weary of him and am glad

163

that Mademoiselle Savy is so willing to take him off my hands!"

With her chin high, she looked defiantly round the company with sparkling eyes, daring anyone to disagree before, with a toss of her golden curls, she left the room, closing the door behind her with a distinct snap.

"Well!" exclaimed Mary Witherspoon, sinking into a chair. "I was never more puzzled in my life! I quite thought—do not tell me I was mistaken, for I am *certain* I am not. How my dearest Clarissa must feel—and really so thoughtless of Kit, whom you know always had the sweetest of manners. To bring that young female here, when we all thought . . . hanging on his arm for all the world, as if—but then, the French are not so nice as we. And *where*, I ask you, is the child he was bringing?"

Amy sighed and said: "I fear we were all mistaken, in a great many things. There was no child, Miss Witherspoon. Kit rescued Mademoiselle Savy and appears to have fallen in love with her at first sight."

"But, Clarissa—!"

"Clarissa assures us that all she ever felt for Kit was fond friendship—and we must believe her."

"Oh, no, no! Her heart will be broken—"

"Nothing of the kind and to say so, Miss Witherspoon, will do Clarissa no good," put in Amy loudly. "You saw how she behaved. Perfectly properly—I daresay that she and Mademoiselle Savy will become the greatest of friends—in fact, that would be the ideal way of stilling any gossip, for you know there are bound to be unkind folk eager to bandy her name around. And now, if you will excuse me—"

She found Clarissa in her room and was relieved to see that she appeared quite calm. "That's my brave girl," she said encouragingly, eliciting a weary smile. "Now—we must plan our strategy. You, my dear, must give every sign of welcoming her, while treating Kit with a degree of indifference."

"*Kit!*" cried Clarissa in tones of loathing. "How could I have thought I— Why, he's no better than a—a *flirt!*"

"How lucky that he betrayed his true character before you committed yourself."

The girl grew still, her expression stricken. "Oh, Aunt Almeria," she murmured. "I didn't hide my feelings. I shall be a laughingstock, for nothing can be more amusing than a jilted heiress!"

"No, no. Nothing of the kind," said Amy soothingly. "I have a plan that will make people think that they were mistaken, and in a short while, all will be forgotten. You must cultivate Marie's friendship."

Clarissa's brows suddenly drew mulishly together, forcibly reminding Amy of Sir Hugo, and she hurried on before the girl could speak. "If you are seen to take her under your wing, nothing could be calculated to stifle speculation quicker."

"No!"

"Introduce her to your friends—"

"No."

"Show Kit that if he even faintly supposed that you wore the willow for him, he was quite mistaken." Her charge looked thoughtful and was silent. "I am persuaded that you will not wear your heart on your sleeve for all to see. It really would be the most foolish thing, my dear . . . and so very

165

gratifying to Master Kit's vanity, for we all know that nothing so feeds a man's ego as a personable female languishing after him!"

"I'd like to—to—*stick pins* in him, the odious, rackety clodpoll!" Clarissa suddenly exclaimed viciously, her pretty face transformed by a snarl. "Why, he's nothing but a—a paltry fellow!"

Amy nodded her approval. "A fickle muttonhead—a regular rattlepate, a ramshackle flirt!" she supplied encouragingly and for a few moments the ladies enjoyed insulting the absent man with all the epithets they knew, but could not normally use.

"I do so hope his ears are burning like beacons," remarked Clarissa, her eyes bright.

Privately Amy doubted it, but did not say so, instead suggesting that if a supper-dance for the younger set was given by Sir Hugo and hosted by Clarissa, under the aegis of Mrs. Masters, to introduce the French girl to society, it would put the final touch to their scheme.

The younger girl's eyes widened. "Aunt Almeria, you have such *good* ideas!" she cried. "How very glad I am that I had the good fortune to find you in that inn. It would be above all things marvelous—none of my friends have had a supper-dance—only the most shabby affairs, you know. Like birthday teas and standing up for country dances with music played by the governess. I could have a new gown ... and put that French miss's nose out of joint." She brooded silently for a second before looking up to ask hopefully: "Do you think Hugo will agree? Once again, dearest Aunt, you are my only hope! Oh, *do* say you'll persuade him."

"I will do my best," Amy promised, and kept her

word later that day, when she slipped downstairs and tapped on the study door a little before the hour for dinner, a time when she knew that Sir Hugo was most likely to be alone.

Already dressed in evening clothes, he rose to his feet as she entered. "A social call, Cousin?" he asked, holding a chair for her.

"N-not really," she replied and saw his eyebrows draw together. "You may have heard of the contretemps here this afternoon?" She looked up at him anxiously and when he shook his head, continued: "As you are aware, Mrs. Masters intended bringing Mademoiselle Savy to visit, which she did this afternoon." Amy had spoken calmly, but now she could restrain her indignation no longer and burst into impassioned speech. "Oh, Sir Hugo, you may imagine poor Clarissa's mortification for, far from being a little child, Marie Savy was a very attractive young lady, chic and elegant as only the French can be and hanging on Kit's arm in what I can only describe as a very possessive way!"

"Good God!" ejaculated Sir Hugo.

"And Kit was very clearly besotted with her."

"The deuce he was!" He looked at Amy keenly. "And is my sister heartbroken—or is merely her pride damaged?"

Miss Standish considered. "She is very shocked. On looking out of the window, her astonishment was great. I believe that she truly thought herself in love with the lieutenant . . . but tend to think that she was more in love with romance. At that age, you know, one is vulnerable to a handsome face in a smart uniform."

"I will take your word for it, never having been susceptible myself."

Amy gazed at him darkly for a moment. "In your case, sir, it would have been a pair of pretty eyes, or an elegant ankle!"

Sir Hugo nodded blandly. "Pray go on. How did Clary take this? With a wild outcry and a show of strong hysterics, I suppose."

"You wrong her. She behaved impeccably. Indeed you must have been proud of her had you been here," she told him roundly. "She greeted them calmly, gave them tea, and conversed with the ease of a hostess double her age and experience."

"I'd lay wager that it was your doing."

"Only after they had gone and in the privacy of her own room did she give vent to her feelings and declare that she would like to stick pins into some unspecified part of Kit's anatomy!"

Sir Hugo laughed. "I believe she will recover."

"Yes—but you must know that she has been somewhat unwise in her certainty of his affection and unfortunately made plain her own attachment. I am sure you will wish to avoid any gossip or speculation that she has been jilted."

"Precisely. What had you in mind?"

Glancing up, Amy found his gaze fixed on her face. "I pointed out to her the advisability of appearing totally indifferent to Kit's amour and took it upon myself to suggest that she should take Marie Savy under her wing. To be seen happily together would be just the thing to stay any rumors of a rift between the families."

"Just so—well put, Cousin. I hope you also pointed out how Kit's vanity would suffer. Tell me, do you suppose that that young man was truly such a numskull as to be unaware of Clarissa's feelings toward him? I would choose to believe so, rather than to think he intended to play fast and loose with her affections."

"They were both undoubtedly enjoying a youthful flirtation, which Clarissa took more seriously than he ... but, I *think* that if he had not met Mademoiselle Savy then, most probably he and Clarissa would have become serious—whether it would have been a good match had you allowed it to proceed, I have my doubts. However, he met Marie Savy under romantic circumstances that made a susceptible young man certain to lose his heart. I am sure that Clarissa, though she doesn't realize it, is more annoyed than hurt and a little distraction will soon restore her spirits."

"What had you in mind?" Sir Hugo asked warily.

Amy shot him a glance and finding his lazy gaze held a degree of amusement, was encouraged to answer promptly. "A supper-dance for the younger set. Although she is not out yet, there could be no impropriety in such an affair, especially if she and Mrs. Masters were to host it jointly in order to introduce Marie Savy to local society. It would certainly have the effect of quelling the most malicious of tongues!"

With one arm stretched along the mantelpiece, Sir Hugo stared down into the depths of the fire. "Very well," he said. "I almost begin to regret rusticating my sister. I realize now how quiet was my life when she consorted with her cronies in London, leaving me to my own devices."

Which is what he told her when, hearing the news, Clarissa forgot her lovelorn state and jumped up from the dinner table to bestow on him a grateful hug and kiss. Drawing her to his side in a rare show of affection, he promised to foot the bill for a

169

new gown. "Mind though, puss," he warned, "this is your affair. I will not be bothered by trivialities—if you require anything, Mr. Fifield will arrange it."

Clarissa swallowed and looked doubtfully across the table to his secretary, who smiled encouragingly. "We will manage," he assured her, having no difficulty in understanding her fears.

"Be guided in all things," added her brother, suddenly struck by all that youthful enthusiasm might propose and feeling that some restraint was wise.

"Dearest of brothers, I give you my word that you will not be incommoded in the slightest," she promised readily. "Only agree that we will not be confined to country dances. For you know that to be forever dancing round and round is the shabbiest thing and not at all fashionable."

"Indeed no," he agreed amiably. "A cotillion or a quadrille is considerably more dashing."

"The waltz is quite acceptable nowadays—" she put in hopefully.

Sir Hugo shook his head.

"Nothing could be more proper," she protested.

"No, Clary—it would not do," he told her firmly, and reading the finality in his voice aright, she did not argue, falling instead into a discussion as to the most suitable date. Eventually the twelfth of April was settled upon as being a few days after Easter, but while people were still in a mood for festivities.

The next day Amy drove Clarissa over to Carley Weston for the purpose of informing Mrs. Masters of Sir Hugo's intention and of persuading her to lend her name to the affair.

"I think it the most delightful idea—and truly kind of Sir Hugo to suggest it." She pressed Amy's

170

hand meaningly, adding quietly: "Though, I feel sure that you, dear Miss Standish, had much to do with it. I shall be honored, indeed, to stand beside my dearest Clarissa, but let me tell you I have no intention of usurping her role of hostess. I am sure that Sarah will be thrilled at the prospect of her first formal dance. I declare that it will give everyone quite a lift of spirits!"

As they took their leave, Amy noticed that Kit maneuvered the opportunity to have a few words with Clarissa but, despite her bright eyes and hectic cheeks, made no comment as they drove away, instead waiting for her to speak if she would.

"Well, of all things!" her charge duly exclaimed indignantly when they were well on the road home. "Kit had the gall to hope that his affection for me had not led *me* into mistaking his intentions!"

"I hope you thought of a suitable set-down."

Clarissa smothered an angry snicker. "I told him that, on the contrary, I felt guilty to have practiced my flirtations on him! That I had always regarded him as a brother and now was more than willing to accept Mademoiselle as a sister." She reflected a moment. "I could have said a great deal more—"

"I think that was perfect," Amy assured her, tooling the light carriage round a bend in the lane, and received a sunny smile in return.

"Yes, it was, was it not? I do not think that my heart can have been broken, for I am quite looking forward to my supper-dance and do not feel at all inclined to pine and waste away!"

"Very sensible," commented her companion, adding casually after a minute: "Whom do you intend to invite? I think Mr. Gambrill can hardly be left out, living as he does in the same household. The unfortunate fact is that there is usually a sad lack of men. . . . Do you consider Sir Simon to be too old?"

Clarissa turned her head quickly. "Not at all— Oh, I see you are funning. Will he care to come, do you think? After all, he may consider it too unsophisticated for his tastes."

"I am sure he will be among the first to accept," reassured Amy, aware of the unconsciously wistful note in the younger woman's voice.

"I do hope so—one is so comfortable with him and somehow never has the least urge to get into scrapes. He and Hugo will add consequence to the affair—after all, to only have young folk would give it the appearance of a *nursery* dance!"

Hiding a smile, Amy drove on, thinking that Clarissa was displaying a degree of interest in Sir Simon that would gratify that gentleman greatly, if only he had the felicitation of knowing of it.

High on the agenda was a trip into Winchester to arrange for new gowns. Having spent very little of her handsome wages, Amy was in the happy position of being able to afford one of Madame Jeanne's creations, and Clarissa had been given free rein by Sir Hugo; and even Miss Witherspoon had been persuaded to add to her somewhat eccentric wardrobe.

Amy already had a style in mind and when she saw a bolt of gold-colored silk, she knew that it was the very thing for the slim, plain gown she yearned for. Following her thoughts without difficulty, Madame Jeanne quickly produced a white, gold-figured gauze for an over-tunic, and Amy sighed with satisfaction.

Clarissa had fallen into raptures over a spangled

muslin, and soon settled upon an underskirt of the palest yellow. Well satisfied with their joint decisions, Amy looked round to see how Miss Witherspoon was managing and found to her dismay that she had decided upon the mustard-colored grosgrain that Clarissa had pined for on their previous visit to the dressmaker's establishment.

To all her alternative suggestions, the governess turned a deaf ear, stroking the grosgrain and preening in the mirror as she held it against herself.

"So very fashionable, you know—indeed quite the 'pink,' if you will allow me to use such a term! Such a delightful color—so bright and gay." She twittered to herself, leaning closer to whisper confidingly in Amy's ear. "I daresay I shall be thought 'all the crack'!" Seeing the doubt in her companion's eyes, she lost her glow. "You do not think it too young?" she asked anxiously, smoothing the material with a loving hand.

Taking pity on her, Amy shook her head. "Not at all. You will quite put us in the shade," she told her truthfully and suggested tactfully that cream trimmings would be more tasteful than the deep purple favored by Miss Witherspoon.

"I only hope that Marie Savy will not outshine us all," observed Clarissa darkly as Tedbury drove out of town. "One cannot help but wonder where her clothes came from. I am sure that they are not what we should consider suitable—after all, she can only be of my age."

"I am not at all old-fashioned, as you know but— A little *too* smart! Her décolleté quite put me to the blush . . . not at all what we consider— So very foreign looking. I wish that Mrs. Masters would have—" agreed Miss Witherspoon.

"I believe that she brought them with her," put in Amy. "Mrs. Masters told me that she arrived with a great deal of luggage."

Clarissa stared at her. "You mean that Kit allowed her to travel with trunks! Well—he must truly be in love, for of all things he hates to be weighed down with baggage. Why, his mama always complains about his high-handedness, and he would not allow poor Sarah to bring her new bonnet when she visited me in London. Whatever he said, it was *not* as high as a bird cage, I assure you." She brooded darkly for a few minutes. "What was she doing with trunks? It all sounds very odd to me."

"I believe that she was attempting to get to the coast in the hopes of hiring a boat to cross the Channel. Her mother was English and so she has relatives here."

"It all sounds decidedly fishy to me," announced Clarissa. "I shouldn't be surprised if she were a spy!"

Amy smiled and shook her head. "She has left it a little late—the war is almost over. Sir Hugo says we shall be in Paris soon and then, you know, the war will be at an end."

"An adventuress, then," said Clarissa, abandoning her first idea. An impish grin appeared. "If I were not a nice girl, I would think it just what Kit deserved," she observed hopefully.

CHAPTER TEN

The ladies had no sooner arrived home and begun to climb the staircase than the rumble of an approaching vehicle caused them to pause and wait expectantly as the butler proceeded at a stately pace across the hall again. Before he could open the door, the bell was jangled imperiously, filling the house with a harsh cacophony of sound. Hill was startled out of his usual calm, jerking the door on its hinges in his surprise at the mistreatment of the bellpull.

Having done her best to deafen the inhabitants of the house, a tall, gaunt female stepped aside and a very large lady, clad in a voluminous traveling cloak, her head enveloped in the hooped folds of an old-fashioned calash, took her place. Lifting a lorgnette, she surveyed the transfixed occupants of the hall.

"Good Heavens—Great-Aunt Augusta!" exclaimed Clarissa faintly, in tones expressive of the greatest dismay and astonishment.

Her voice attracted the basilisk gaze of the new arrival, who raised her eyeglass again to stare at her great-niece. "Come down here at once, girl," she commanded, brushing aside the hovering form of Mr. Hill as if he had been no more than an annoying midge.

Showing decided reluctance, Clarissa slowly descended the stairs, creeping past Amy, who followed her, feeling that her charge definitely had need of moral support.

"G-Great-Aunt, how pleasant to see you," quavered Clarissa. "D-did you send notice of your arrival? If so, I am afraid it must have gone astray—you find us quite at sixes and sevens, and Hugo is not here—"

"I came," intoned her aunt in a majestic voice, "in answer to a rumor!"

"Oh! Well, I cannot think how you could have heard, especially when we have been at such pains to keep it secret," Clarissa declared indignantly, thinking she knew the reason for the unexpected visit. "And really, such a visit will only serve to make matters worse!"

Lady Myers turned to the interested butler and commanded that he and his minion take themselves off, before bestowing a withering glance upon the wilting Clarissa. "So you are in on the sordid affair—I own to astonishment! By all that is marvelous, I am positively astounded that Hugo is so far gone in all that's nice as to involve his young sister in impropriety!" Having effectively silenced her niece, the formidable lady raised her eyeglass again to examine Amy, a pained expression on her haughty features.

Finding herself the object of a freezing scrutiny from the hideously enlarged orb, Amy instinctively lifted her chin and frowned, bewildered by the animosity of the unexpected guest.

"How do you do, ma'am," she said, determined not to be shaken.

"I did not hear you address me!" was the surprising response. Pulling back her extraordinary headgear to reveal the folds of an antiquated mauve satin turban, Lady Myers bridled unmistakably. "I have not seen you—you, young woman, do not exist!"

Clarissa stared blankly from one to the other, nonplussed, until finally she decided that her great-aunt had taken leave of her senses. "Was the journey very bad?" she asked solicitously. "We will have a hot brick put in your bed and you will feel much better after a little rest— But first let me introduce Miss Standish. Aunt Almeria, this is Lady Myers, Grandpapa's sister—"

She got no further, for the large woman uttered a snort of rage and pawed the ground with one large booted foot, rather in the manner of an enraged bull. "So—the rumors are true!" she bellowed. "Aunt Almeria, indeed! Do you think to fool me, child, when I know every twist and turn of the family's lineage. There is *no* Almeria, aunt or otherwise, among the Dysarts! I should have thought better of Hugo than to try to foist his inamorata on us in this way—and with his sister and nevvy in the same house! It's not decent! I don't know what the world's coming to, 'deed I don't!"

Amy could only stare blankly at the furious face that had become an alarming shade of puce. "I—have no idea what you mean," she ventured at last, "but let me advise you to calm yourself, ma'am, for fear of an apoplexy!"

The furious female took so deep a breath that her bosom appeared to double in size, but whatever she

177

intended to say remained forever unsaid, for at that moment, Sir Hugo walked through the front door, which Hill had forgotten to close, and surveyed the scene before him calmly.

"Aunt Augusta, how unexpected to see you," he remarked, pulling off his riding gloves. "Of course your visits are always a pleasure, but I am at a loss as to what can have persuaded you to leave Town."

"Nephew!" she enunciated awfully, making full use of the breath she had not so far used. "Are you so forgetful of your position as to install your light-of-love in Candover Magna?"

Sir Hugo's black eyebrows snapped together, but either ignoring or unaware of the danger sign, Lady Myers, now that she was in full flow, plunged on. "I am not mealymouthed. Others may whisper behind their hands; I will say it straight out. *It will not do,* Hugo! To bring your high-flyer here— Good God, man, you are old enough to know how to go on."

"Enough, Aunt!" Sir Hugo cut across her. He spoke quietly but with authority enough to silence the angry woman. "It puzzles me, Aunt, where you learn such terms. I can only suppose that your cronies are not up to scratch! With regard to your totally unfounded surmises, we all will pretend that we have not heard them." He glanced meaningly round at the stunned members of his family, before going to the foot of the stairs and holding out his hand to Amy. "Will you be so understanding as to forgive a foolish old lady?" he asked, with a steely glance at his aunt. "I am afraid that our secret must be revealed," he went on, taking her cold fingers in a warm grip and impelling her to descend the stairs. When she stood beside him, he contin-

178

ued: "Aunt Augusta, let me introduce my fiancée to you. Miss Amy Standish."

The room spun round Amy and her hand quivered in his grasp. "My love," Sir Hugo continued, astonishingly, "I know you will forgive my aunt her misunderstanding. I am assured that only her great love of family could have persuaded her into such indiscretion." Under his austere gaze Lady Myers seemed to shrivel somewhat, losing some of her high color and much of her bombastic manner. "Precisely so," he said, accepting the apology that would never be spoken. "If you will look up the stairs, you will see Miss Witherspoon, who has been so kind as to act as duenna, so you need have no fear for our good name."

He tugged at the bellrope hanging beside the fireplace and Hill appeared in answer suspiciously quickly. "Ah, Hill, I see you had the commonsense not to retire too far," remarked his lordship acidly. "Pray desire Mrs. Hill to ready the green bedchamber for Lady Myers and have a tea tray sent to the withdrawing room."

The butler bowed. "I have taken the liberty of already doing so. I thought it was what you would wish, sir," he said urbanely. "If her ladyship's abigail will follow the footman, she will find all in readiness."

The tall woman who had rung the doorbell sniffed and glanced at her mistress, who made an irritated gesture of dismissal.

"Yes, yes. Off you go, Mesham."

"Let me take your ladyship's calash and cloak," ventured the maid, pulling at the various fastenings to her mistress's clothes.

"Don't fuss me, Mesham," cried Lady Myers,

slapping at her hovering hand. Untying the strings, she threw her head covering and cloak back from her shoulders without waiting to see that they were caught and sailed across the hall to the drawing room. "Well, Nevvy, come and keep me company," she commanded. Fixing Amy with a rather protuberant gray eye, she crooked her finger. "You too, Miss—whatever your name is," she added, and marched through the doorway.

Somewhat to her surprise, Amy discovered that her hand was still fast in Sir Hugo's grip and, unable to put the emotions she felt into words, sent that gentleman a speaking look.

"Forgive me," he said, smiling down into her eyes in a way that made her suddenly breathless. "This is not how I wished it to be—" Breaking off abruptly, he, too, seemed at a loss for the appropriate word. "But—but believe me when I say that all will be as you wish it. Trust me, Amy. I give you my word."

Amy could only shake her head. "I do not understand," she murmured, rubbing at the perplexed frown that crossed her forehead. "Surely—surely you do not *wish* to be engaged to me? How could you?" She searched his face.

"Very easily," he told her reassuringly. "All will be well, I promise. Later we will talk. . . ."

"Your aunt's accusations have caused you to make this announcement out of a misplaced sense of chivalry—you think to save me from embarrassment—" She spoke rather wildly, in a distraught manner.

Sir Hugo had been jolted into the announcement, which had surprised himself as much as his listeners, by sheer fury at his aunt's behavior. Surprised

180

by the strength of his feelings upon seeing Miss Standish white-faced under Lady Myers's attack, Sir Hugo had been filled with the urge to protect her, to his own astonishment! Tucking her trembling hand into the crook of his elbow and holding it there in a comforting grip, he said: "Bear with me. Later, should you so wish, you may cry off."

Convinced that she was being used to teach the termagant a lesson, Amy flushed miserably; but while she sought desperately for some way out of the predicament in which she found herself, Clarissa, who had been struck dumb and motionless by her brother's unexpected announcement, hurtled down the remaining stairs and flung herself upon Sir Hugo.

"Hugo, Hugo! By all that's wonderful!" she cried, hugging him. "Nothing could make me happier—I declare that I've been aware of an interest on your part for some time, but never thought you'd come to the point for some time yet." She turned to Amy and kissed her heartily, never noticing the other's reticence. "And what a sly boots you are, Aunt Almeria. How delightful! To be honest, I never thought I'd be grateful to Great-Aunt, for she is forever upsetting things usually, but I must own that she has proved most useful. Without her rudeness sending you into a huff, Hugo, we all would have had to wait to hear your happy news, for Heaven knows how long!"

She beamed from Amy to her brother, clasping her hands and almost dancing with barely suppressed joy. Behind her Mary Witherspoon gathered her own scattered wits and trotted down the stairs, talking all the while.

"Dear Sir Hugo, my felicitations—always the romantic! Miss Standish, pray allow me to wish you happy—to be sure the thought never entered my head. A secret betrothal—for all the world like a novel. How surprised everyone—quite a nine days' wonder, I daresay. . . . *The Times*—I never think it quite official until I read it there—you'll think me silly, I know—"

"Miss Standish and I will discuss the matter later," Sir Hugo said firmly. "We have a great deal to decide." He raised Amy's hand to his lips and kissed her fingers lightly. "Now, if you are agreeable, let us go and confront my formidable relative, if you please."

A few minutes earlier Amy would have refused, but something Clarissa had said had given her cause for thought; upon occasion she had wondered herself if Sir Hugo had shown an interest. A few times she had been aware that his gaze held a degree of warmth that was unexpected. Could, she wondered, *could* he care for her? Was it possible that a man in his position would even notice his sister's companion? For some time she had known that her own affections were engaged, but aware of her lowly position and knowing only too well that most employers regarded their dependents as almost another species, she had schooled herself to accept that her feeling, which never could be reciprocated, should not be admitted, even to herself. But now . . . Looking up with dawning hope, she found Sir Hugo smiling down at her, a hint of anxiety in his gray eyes. The totally unexpected sign of vulnerability made her heart miss a beat.

"Shall we pay our dues to my aunt?" he asked and upon Amy nodding, led the way.

"You took long enough," that lady remarked as

they entered. Sipping her tea loudly, she regarded them over the rim of the cup.

"Of course, Aunt, as head of this family, I will give you all respect due," her nephew told her. "I am sure that you know, as well as I, that I need answer to no one."

Gray eyes regarded him thoughtfully and a sound very like a snort escaped her. "Cutting up fine, Nevvy?" she asked. "Well—I daresay you are right. Should have known that you're too aware of your own consequence to install your bit of muslin in the family seat! Too stiff-necked, by far!" She nodded her head as if the matter was settled before turning her gaze on Amy. "Come and let me look at you," she commanded. "Well," she commented, having studied her from head to heel, "you're a nice enough looking girl. I like your air of elegance. I take it you're one of the Hertfordshire Standishes? Though you can't be one of Bella's girls—I know for a fact that they're all bucktoothed to a degree!"

Amy lifted her chin. "I, ma'am, am a nobody," she announced coldly.

A smothered chuckle came from Sir Hugo. "I have it on good authority that Miss Standish is The Only Hope."

Lady Myers displayed an interest. "One of the Hopes, is she? Can't think what you mean by the only one, for they have always proliferated like rabbits!" She nodded her head at Amy. "Don't think I don't know when I'm being roasted—however, you're a taking little thing, not just in the ordinary way, and will not disgrace the Dysarts, if I'm any judge of character. I'll let folk know that the match has my blessing—"

"Too kind," murmured her nephew, causing her

to shoot a sharp stare in his direction. "Knowing how valued is your time, Aunt, am I to take it that you intend to stay a few days?" he continued blandly, with the faintest of emphasis on the "few."

Something rather resembling a grin crossed her ladyship's features, vividly betraying her Dysart kinship. "Don't think to be rid of me that easily, Hugo," she said. "Think I'd leave without looking over my old home? I intend to see how you are managing the Manor, Nevvy, and maybe give you a word or two of advice."

Sir Hugo bowed. "How disappointed I would be if you did not!"

Lady Myers snorted. "Do not think to gammon me," she retorted briskly, obviously enjoying the exchange. "I'm not one of your lovelorn maidens yearning for a pretty word. I am well aware of the feelings the sight of my coach arouses among my kin. I know precisely what you thought as you entered the hall."

"That, Aunt Augusta, I doubt very much."

A chuckle shook her large frame. "You always were my favorite nephew—never could abide toadeaters—or folk who let me ride roughshod over them! Never did care for lily-livered crawlers—talking of whom, where's Lucius? I've a word or two for that gentleman."

Sir Hugo surveyed his aunt. "I rather thought you might," he observed. "I take it he was your source of information."

"Well, of all the infamous things!" cried Amy, outraged. "He must be well aware that I am not a high-flyer!" Suddenly aware of the silence her outburst had provoked, she bit her lip as she glanced from one to the other of the faces turned in her direction. "Oh, dear—I should not have said that. I am afraid that one stores up such phrases and—they pop out unexpectedly."

"Rest assured that *I* do not think the worse of you. Hugo is no mealymouthed individual either." Her ladyship sent a shrewd glance at her nephew, who was standing lost in thought. "Now, Nevvy, take that black look off your face. Lucius did no more than tell me the truth—that a female unknown to the family had taken up residence here and appeared to be on excellent terms with you, allowing me to draw my own conclusions."

"Lucius has an almost impressive talent for slipping in a poisoned word."

"I fancy he's jealous."

"Of me?" Sir Hugo's eyebrows rose in surprise.

"Of your position and wealth."

He gave a short laugh. "I've had to work for it! Lucius is not poor. The fellow's forever talking about his sugar plantations and boasting of his riches—only the other day he ordered a coat from Weston and that, my dear Aunt, costs more than a penny!"

Lady Myers was slowly shaking her head. "That's not what his mama writes in her letters. He's here on the lookout for a wealthy wife to save the family fortunes!"

Having drained the last of the tea from the pot, Lady Myers felt called upon to point out that Amy was not wearing her nephew's ring and removed herself from the room in order to rest before dinner, and Sir Hugo and Amy were left alone. Miss Standish found something of inordinate interest in the garden and gave all her attention to staring out of the window. The silence grew unbearable and at last she sent Sir Hugo a glance from under her lashes, to her discomfort finding him regarding her intently, his face grave.

"Are you annoyed?" he asked unexpectedly.

This was a question she had not expected to be asked and her eyes flew to his face. "Annoyed?" she repeated, savoring the word. "No. That is not my emotion. Amazed, shaken . . . astonished—"

He came to join her in the window embrasure. "But—not angry or dismayed?" he asked.

"Oh, sir, why did you do it?" she cried suddenly. "I did not deserve to be used to discompose your aunt!"

"You have very little faith in me, if you truly think that I would behave in so despicable a fashion."

She moved impatiently. "What am I to think? That you have been hiding a *tendre* for me?"

She allowed her distress to show and he took her hand and held it in a firm grasp. "When I came in to find my aunt berating you, I own to a wild desire to take her by her throat and shake the life from her," he said with suppressed violence.

"I see—so, knowing that this was unacceptable, you decided to surprise her into an apoplexy," Amy observed, striving for cool lightness, but only achieving a brittle bitterness.

Sir Hugo carried her hand to his mouth and kissed the back of her fingers. "I announced the only thing that gave me the right to protect you," he told her gently. "Forgive me for the manner— but, I have never been in such a position before. You would make me very happy if you will accept my offer of marriage."

Amy gazed up at him, her quickened breath fluttering the lace of her high collar. "You are teasing me, I know. You do not care for me—you cannot want to marry me," she announced positively, trying in vain to release her hand. "You can have your choice of any female of wealth and good birth. You must know that I have neither."

"At six-and-thirty, I am still unwed and the despair of every matchmaking mama. No well-bred heiress has ever appealed to me. I own to being difficult to please—" He smiled down into her eyes and possessing himself of both her hands, held them against the breast of his blue superfine coat. "I am convinced that you, Amy, are my only hope. Do not, I pray, disappoint me!"

The familiar name and the fondly teasing note in his voice did more to convince Amy of his sincerity than any impassioned plea of love could have done and she raised her wondering eyes to meet his.

"Amy," he cried, reading her gaze, and swept her into his embrace. "I have never met a female like you—you have surprised, annoyed, intrigued, and amused me by turn. With your calm common sense, your sense of fun, you have enlivened the gloom of the Manor—even managing to tame Clarissa, changing her from an infuriating and silly schoolgirl into a pleasant young woman. I strongly suspect that we all cannot manage without you!"

"D-do you love me?" she dared to ask, afraid of his answer yet knowing that she could never accept his proposal without his affection.

Tipping her head back, he looked into her eyes, allowing her to read his own. "I need you—the day I do not see you I consider wasted. It pleases me when you come into a room . . . the idea of you leaving here is unbearable—is that love? Never having

187

felt it before, I do not know from experience, but I suspect it is so."

Miss Standish sighed and nestled closer. "Oh, yes," she replied confidently, "that's exactly love."

As her head was still tilted and her lips temptingly near, he bent his head and kissed her, a proceeding that Amy found profoundly satisfying.

"I'll send the family betrothal ring to your room," he told her, "in the hope that people will think it needed to be altered to fit and now has arrived back from the silversmith."

He was as good as his word, and a short while later, answering a knock at her door, Amy found Mr. Fifield in the corridor, proffering a small, leather box.

"May I present my best wishes," he said formally. "I hope you will be very happy."

Amy thanked him, remembering that, at one time, she had suspected his own interest was fixed on her, and he bowed gravely before turning and walking along the corridor.

Closing the door, she took the box to the window before opening it. Taking out the thick band of gold that held a large cabochon ruby in an antique setting, she slipped it on her finger and turned her hand this way and that to catch the light. The ring felt heavy and unfamiliar on her finger, making her realize that the happenings of the last few hours had not been a dream, and she abruptly sat down on the window seat to consider the astonishing position in which she found herself.

She had not been there long and had not had time to collect her thoughts when, after the briefest of taps, Clarissa burst into the room.

"Aunt Almeria!" she cried. "What a sly boots you

are! I was never more surprised in my life than when Hugo made his announcement as cool as a cucumber—though, to be sure, now I look back, I can clearly see that you have long had an understanding. I *wondered* what kept him at the Manor, and was amazed at the sweetness of his temper! You have done him good, for, to own the truth, I have never liked him half so well." She gave Amy a hearty kiss and continued happily. "How delightful it will be to have you as a sister." She reflected for a moment before pronouncing gloomily that the only pity was that now Great-Aunt Augusta was sure to stay. "She will insist upon taking charge of everything—even my supper-dance."

How right she was, the ladies found out when, descending to the dining room, they discovered Lady Myers and her nephew already arguing about the notice to be sent to *The Times*.

"Mr. Fifield will do all that is necessary," said the baronet with finality. "By all means give *Clarissa* your experience and advice, but I beg of you, remember it is her occasion and the experience of making the arrangements herself will prove invaluable to her in the future."

Admitting defeat, Lady Myers gave in gracefully. "Clarissa, my dear child, call upon me for anything. I have some charming ideas, entirely suitable for a young people's affair."

Clarissa smiled dutifully, unable to hide her doubts, but Lady Myers proved surprisingly helpful and amenable, sharing her experience gathered from hosting many such functions over her long life, giving answers to various questions that arose, and supplying several ideas that would raise the dance above the ordinary.

"Do you know," Clarissa remarked thoughtfully the day before the event, "I own to being quite surprised. I always thought Aunt Augusta old-fashioned in the extreme, with those strange quizzes of hats she wears, but her ideas have been bang-up to the nines! What could be more enchanting than that rustic bower she caused Mr. Hodge to construct for the orchestra, and he is such a curmudgeonly man, and how I *wish* Hugo had not been so small-minded as to refuse to allow us to have a waterfall in the ballroom—even Mr. Hodge was quite taken with the prospect, once it had been explained to him. I am persuaded that nothing could have been more charming!"

"More wet, you mean," was Amy's dry reply. "How could you have danced on a damp floor, you goose? And it's all very well to say that the water would not have escaped, but it would, you know, and only think how furious your guests would have been if their shoes were ruined, besides how ridiculous they would have looked in their stocking feet! Be grateful for the delights of the bower and take my advice not to put your brother in bad fettle by making outrageous demands."

Clarissa obviously privately agreed with this and, giving a sunny smile, desisted from her most wild flights of fancy, instead speculating upon the gowns the guests would be wearing.

"Whatever Mademoiselle is wearing, I am convinced that nothing could be more becoming than the gown Madame Jeanne has made for me," she declared complacently.

Amy, who had been allowed a glimpse of the sparkling, fairy-tale concoction, agreed, adding that she, herself, intended to cut a pretty figure.

Clarissa eyed her critically. "Now that you have left off your spectacles and those horrid caps you wore, you look quite the thing," she told her. "When I first saw you in that inn, I took you to be quite middle-aged, but with your hair arranged in that softer way, you look to be not much past the flush of youth."

"Why, thank you, Clarissa dear," Amy returned with a hint of irony.

"Oh, I do not mean that you are *old*," said her charge teasingly, "but you must admit to having been out of leading strings for some time!"

"Wait until tomorrow—I intend to do my best to outshine you all," promised Amy with a smile, and the next evening, when she looked at the elegant, fashionably dressed woman gazing coolly back at her, she knew that she had kept her word.

Lady Myers's maid had been persuaded to lend her talents to arrange her hair, and under her clever fingers, Amy's soft brown curls had been coaxed into a style that flattered her green eyes and delicate features. Sir Hugo's betrothal present had been a pair of gold-and-diamond drop earrings, and moving her head, Amy spent a pleasant few moments in admiring the way the candlelight struck sparks on them before, collecting her long gloves and fan, lent by Clarissa, she left her room to make her way, not without trepidation, down to the hall where the family was gathering to meet their guests.

Meeting Clarissa coming out of her room, they each paused to admire the other.

"Why, Aunt Almeria—you look beautiful!" exclaimed the younger woman with genuine pleasure.

"Thank you, Clary," Amy responded, aware of

looking her best. "I am sure that you will be the belle of the ball. I only hope that you may not break too many hearts!"

Arriving in the hall, they found that the gentlemen were already there and that Hodge, the gardener, had surpassed himself with the floral tributes he had arranged for each lady; white violets and primroses complemented Amy's gown, making her suspect that he had had the services of the indoor staff; pale pink dianthus in a cloud of white gypsophila awaited Clarissa. Mary Witherspoon exclaimed delightedly over a spray of mauve and yellow heartsease, while Lady Myers was already pinning a corsage of violets to her impressive purple bosom.

Reading the admiration in Sir Hugo's eyes, Amy blushed a little as he presented the posy to her with a bow. Taking her hand, he carried it to his lips before expressing his pleasure at her appearance.

Dropping into a curtsy, she smiled up at him, her bright eyes sparkling with anticipation. "What fun this is," she could not help saying, her excitement clear to see, all her former nerves forgotten. "How delightful Clarissa looks."

"My sister looks like a princess from a fairy tale. You, my love, have the elegant enchantment due to human beauty," he told her, taking both her hands to raise her from her obeisance.

The hall had been cleared for dancing, wide double doors into the crimson drawing room were pulled back and the furniture removed to clear the floor. Above, in the overhanging gallery, the small orchestra, resplendent in its rustic bower, waited patiently.

As if at a given signal, the musicians began to tune their instruments. Flowers and ferns banked the stairs and a thousand candles struck flashing lights from the newly cleaned crystal drops of the chandeliers.

The family had not long to wait, for scarcely had the ladies taken their places than the rumble of approaching wheels announced the imminent arrival of the first guests and Hill gravely stepped forward, signaling to the pair of footmen, resplendent in their powdered wigs and bright livery, to fling open the front door. . . . Clarissa's supper-dance had begun.

CHAPTER ELEVEN

When the last of the guests were judged to have arrived, Sir Hugo caught the watchful eyes of the leader of the orchestra and the first chord of a country dance was sounded, partners were quickly sought, and the enjoyments of the evening commenced. Penn, who had been allowed to stay up to watch from the balcony the beginning of the exciting events, was persuaded to leave his vantage point and retired reluctantly to bed, with many backward glances.

Lucius partnered Clarissa for the first dance, while Sir Hugo stood up with Mademoiselle Savy, as the occasion was being held in their joint honor.

Amy was watching the performance of her charge with a proprietary air, thinking that the hours of tuition spent teaching Clarissa the steps, while Miss Witherspoon played the pianoforte, had not been wasted, when she became aware of a gentleman at her elbow.

"Miss Standish," murmured Sir Simon, bowing, "I hear you are to be felicitated. Let me wish you happy. Sir Hugo is to be congratulated on his good fortune."

"You are too kind," she replied. "We had not intended to make it public knowledge just yet, but with the dance and Lady Myers arriving ... it suddenly seemed the best of times—"

"It will have come as no surprise to your acquaintances," he told her, his eyes twinkling. "I, for one, have been expecting an announcement."

"You surprise me," she said truthfully, wondering if her feelings had truly been so clear to others. "I must own to being a little disconcerted—I had not thought to be so—so *transparent!*"

"Do not be embarrassed. It was exceedingly pleasant to see two people so happy in each other's company." Above her head, his eyes dwelt on Clarissa, solemnly executing her dance steps, and an indulgent smile curved his lips. "What a delightful child Miss Clarissa is," he remarked. "So sweet-natured and unaffected—who else would share her dance with another female? Especially a foreign beauty with all the kudos a romantic tale bestows." He paused before adding quietly, "I take it that Lieutenant Masters ... That is, that Mademoiselle Savy and he—"

Amy took pity on him. "I assure you that Clarissa's feelings were never firmly fixed," she said. "She is pleased that her childhood friend has found someone worthy of him and was only too happy to be able to give this sign of her pleasure."

Sir Simon smiled down at her. "I understand," he told her. "I do not need to be told that it was at your suggestion, Miss Standish."

"And *I* do not need to tell you, sir, that Clarissa would be particularly glad of an attentive beau!" Amy replied, adding casually that her gown might have been chosen to go with a naval uniform, and after scribbling his initials on her dance card, the

195

lieutenant surrendered his place beside her to Sir Hugo, who was claiming Amy for the next dance.

"It appears to be going well," he remarked, leading her to join the sets that were forming along the length of the hall. "Mademoiselle Savy is a striking female. She quite puts our English maidens in the shade."

Following his gaze to where the French girl was surrounded by a bevy of admirers, Amy nodded. "She carries off that particular shade of sea-green very well—though not many mamas here would approve of her choice of color for so young a girl," she said, thinking that so strong a shade had the effect of rendering the pale muslins of her companions insipid. "Nothing could make Clarissa appear less than beautiful," she added firmly. "How glad I am that she chose that rosy pink!"

"She does not lack partners. When I left her, her card was already full and she was having the pleasure of being able to refuse young Masters as a partner!"

"Oh, good! Nothing could have made her feel better," exclaimed Amy as they waited their turn to take part in the intricate dance.

After that the evening became a whirl of exhaustion, a kaleidoscope of color, and a blur of conversation, all blending together to form enjoyment beyond her expectations. Not short of partners herself, she was glad when Sir Hugo returned to accompany her into supper and sank onto a chair with a sigh of relief while he went off to fill their plates.

By way of novelty, the first dance after the interval was an old-fashioned pavane and Sir Hugo and Lady Myers headed the procession in a stately march around the ground floor of the Manor, gravely bowing or curtsying to all they met on their way, whom, having returned the salute, took their places at the end. At first bemused and uncertain, the younger guests joined in reluctantly but quickly found an unexpected pleasure in the slow, proud progression and grave, stately steps.

During the course of the evening, Amy had kept an eye on Clarissa, hoping her presence would not be needed, but ready to come to her charge's aid should the necessity arise. For some time all seemed well; she caught sight of the gleaming head of blond curls first with one partner and then another, the familiar gurgle of laughter denoting her enjoyment, but after supper Amy became aware that some form of tension had arisen; there was a slight change in the air, several of the younger gentlemen bore signs of irritation, and looking round for the cause, she noticed that Clarissa was dancing with Lucius for the third time, while a youth, who obviously considered it *his* dance, glowered from among the watchers, his arms folded across his yellow waistcoat.

Warned by the mulish droop to Clarissa's mouth and the brilliant sparkle in her eyes, Amy stepped down from her vantage point on the staircase and began to make her way across the hall to the girl, but having to thread her way among the dancers, stopping to speak to any who caught her attention, took some minutes, and by the time she reached where Clarissa and Lucius had been, it was to find no sign of them.

Bewildered for a moment, she looked around rather helplessly until a firm hand took her elbow and a voice murmured in her ear.

197

"They are in the orangery." And with an efficient neatness that she could not but admire, Lieutenant Lovell maneuvered her calmly, in a casual manner that went unnoticed, to the door in the center of the room.

Normally a curtain concealed it, but earlier this had been drawn back and the door opened to let cool air into the overheated hall. Now that door was closed, a fact that made Amy and Sir Simon exchange anxious glances.

As they entered, the sound of a gasp, followed by a loud slap, made them start forward. The area was lighted only by a pair of rather dim lanterns, while the moonlight was well dispersed by a covering of clouds, but they could not mistake the two figures struggling at the far end.

As Sir Simon exclaimed and started forward, Amy caught his sleeve. "No scandal!" she whispered urgently, thinking of Clarissa's reputation.

Patting her hand reassuringly, he walked calmly toward the pair, who had become aware of his presence.

"My dance, I think, Miss Clarissa," he said in a voice that allowed no argument, offering her his arm.

With an angry sob, Clarissa twitched herself out of her cousin's grasp, giving the naval man her hand with obvious relief. "H-how glad I am that you remembered and c-came in search of me!" she said, glaring at Lucius.

"Really, Lucius, I would have expected you to have better care of Clarissa. Even cousins, you know, have to obey the rules," observed Amy easily, coming forward and surprising a look of chagrin on his face. Something of his intentions dawned on her, but controlling her rising anger, she tucked her hand into his elbow and continued comfortably. "How fortunate that Sir Simon and I happened to follow you—we will all go back together and no one will think anything of it."

His arm was stiff and unyielding, but disregarding his obvious reluctance, she propelled him toward the entrance as Sir Simon and Clarissa walked ahead. Casting a glance at her companion as they stepped into the brightly lit hall, she understood his reluctance; a bright red mark disfigured one cheek and his eye was rapidly closing.

"Oh, dear," she said solicitously. "That does look painful! Sir Simon, Clarissa, pray look at poor Lucius. Orangeries are such dangerous places! You could have hurt yourself badly, Lucius. Did you walk into something? Or perhaps something hit you! Take my advice and have more care in the future."

Aware that her voice had drawn the attention of the surrounding guests, he glared at her from his good eye as a babble of amused speculative conversation arose before, turning abruptly, he left the room.

"Mr. Gambrill had the misfortune to walk into something," Amy announced brightly. "I am sure he will have more care in future."

Seeing that Sir Simon had drawn Clarissa aside to a small sofa where, seated beside her, he leaned forward to shield her from unwanted attention, while engaging her in gentle, undemanding conversation, Amy thought with some satisfaction that the outcome of the unfortunate affair might well be to his advantage.

"What's to do?" inquired Sir Hugo, smiling for

199

his guests, but his eyes watchful. "I saw Lucius slinking off with the beginnings of a fine black eye and heard tales of his having walked into something in the orangery. Knowing my orangery very well, I have little fault to find in the story, but suspect that Sir Simon's fist and not an orange branch was the cause."

"I . . . rather think it was Clarissa," murmured Amy. "I believe that Lucius had been paying her unwanted attentions, even to the extent of claiming dances belonging to others. . . . Possibly he took a liberty—"

"The deuce he did!" he exclaimed, surprised into showing his feelings. Quickly recovering his aplomb, he smoothed his features and continued blandly: "How long has this been going on?"

"If you remember, there was the odd affair when Clarissa left Town under his protection . . . and felt herself threatened enough to call on me for aid. The poor girl was doubted then and he carried it off, but if he is on the lookout for a wealthy wife, as Lady Myers suggests, who would suit his purposes better than Clarissa?"

"Good God! And when she turned to me, I thought her acting the part of a vapid, lovelorn female!" Sir Hugo was contrite. "However, he must know that I would never give my consent. I have often made it clear that I do not agree with close kin marrying."

"If his intention was to cause a scandal and he was successful in giving rise to gossip and damaging her reputation, which you must know is the easiest thing, he might well believe that you would think differently."

Sir Hugo was silent, digesting this. "How devious of him," he remarked at last. "I begin to see that there is more to Cousin Lucius than I supposed. I think it is time he ceased to enjoy my hospitality—"

His expression was so grim and he spoke with such finality that Amy felt a pang of sympathy for the hapless Lucius but, before she could say anything, James Fifield appeared at Sir Hugo's elbow to whisper discreetly in his patron's ear. Amy could not hear what was said, but he carried an air of suppressed excitement, so different to his usual unflurried manner, that she felt her heart lurch in anticipation.

Sir Hugo straightened his broad shoulders, giving a heartfelt sigh, his gaze flickering over the dancing throng. Recalling her presence, he turned back to press her hand and say briefly: "The best of news, my dear," before, mounting the stairs, he signaled for the orchestra to stop playing, turning to face his guests in the ensuing silence.

"My friends," he began, as puzzled eyes sought the reason for this interruption to their entertainment. When he had their attention, he repeated his words to Amy. "The best of news— Word has just come from London that the Allies entered Paris on the thirty-first of March!" There was a gasp from his listeners and then a ragged cheer from the men, and raising his voice in order to be heard above the hubbub, he continued loudly: "The Little General—Napoleon Bonaparte abdicated a week ago on the sixth of April."

Whoops, whistles, laughter, and loud speculation filled the hall, and taking its cue from the proud reaction of the guests, the orchestra began to play the national anthem. As the fervent singing died away,

Sir Hugo commanded Hill to provide a toast and threaded his way through the excited, noisy crowd to Amy's side.

"Does this mean that we are at peace?" she asked.

"I pray so—but news travels slowly . . . especially under the present circumstances. With such a divided army, consisting of so many different nationalities, the lines of communication cannot but be confused. For the next few days, I am afraid that anything could happen." Seeing the worried frown that creased her forehead, he smiled down at her, adding reassuringly: "Peace is definitely at hand. There may be a few skirmishes between corps who have not heard the news, but without Napoleon, you may be sure France will not continue the war."

When everyone had a filled glass, Sir Hugo raised his own. "To our fighting men and to our able commander. Ladies and Gentlemen, I give you Field Marshal Wellington and all the men who have fought for us!"

With murmurs of agreement, the toast was echoed; then Mademoiselle Savy leaped up on a chair, beaming round at the somewhat surprised faces upturned to her.

"To ze brave British Army!" she cried, and sending a sparkling glance from her black eyes toward Sir Simon Lovell in his blue uniform, "And to ze jolly Jack Tars!"

Amid concerted indulgent laughter, she drank deeply from her glass before allowing Kit to lift her down.

"Allow me to offer another." Heads turned in Sir Simon's direction, and seeing he had their attention, he went on: "To our brave, if misguided, enemies!"

The toast was drunk with only slightly less enthusiasm, and with an expansive gesture, Sir Hugo commanded the orchestra to strike up again and the evening proceeded, lifted out of the ordinary by the relief and happiness felt by all. Stout matrons and stern duennas were swept into the dance; even Lady Myers attempted a lively cotillion, showing unexpected elegance and lightness of foot.

The hour grew late and eventually the last dance was announced, but as the orchestra prepared to play the first note, the host ran lightly up the stairs and bent to speak to the leader, who nodded and turned to speak to his fellow musicians. Leaning over the gallery railing, Sir Hugo smiled down at his guests.

"I am sure no one will object," he began. "It cannot be denied that this is a momentous occasion, therefore, Ladies and Gentlemen, I announce the last dance! Pray take your partners for a waltz!"

As the orchestra broke into a lilting tune, he hurried down the stairs and swept Amy into the dance. With her hand on his shoulder and his arm around her waist, they circled the hall in perfect union, intensely aware of each other.

"An evening to remember, sir," she observed after a while.

"Precisely so. But now you must learn to call me Hugo."

"H-Hugo," she returned, suddenly shy. "I think that I shall remember this night all my life! I—feel as if it is all a fairy tale. That I shall wake up and find it has been a dream. One moment I am a lowly governess, with only prospects of an impecunious future—then, without the aid of a fairy godmother, I am suddenly—" Unable to express her feelings, she gestured at herself, her surroundings, and the man who held her, *"here,"* she finished inadequately. "I find it hard to believe."

His arm tightened. "Let us hope that there is no wicked fairy about to put in an appearance!" he teased, his eyes gleaming down at her, and taking up her free hand, which was elegantly engaged in holding the skirt of her dress, he kissed it, his lips lingering long enough to make her miss a step.

"I thought she had arrived," Amy admitted, as Lady Myers sailed past, as stately as a ship under full sail, "but found her instead, to be a fairy godmother!"

Hugo laughed. "I've heard Aunt Augusta called many things, but never that."

Sometime later, when the last guest had left, the weary inhabitants of Candover Magna climbed the stairs, all, save one, well pleased with themselves as they retired to bed. Amy's rest was broken by a series of vivid dreams in which witches and other creatures of fairyland much featured, and she awoke unrefreshed. Her first waking thoughts were of the very thing that she had unaccountably allowed to slip her mind, and as her heart sank unpleasantly, she knew that she must face up to the fact that she must make known to Sir Hugo her relationship to the actress, Clorinda Beaufort.

With this in mind, she ventured downstairs, finding the servants busy at work removing all signs of the night's entertainment. A light breakfast was set in the dining room, but of the other occupants of the house there was no sign. Feeling stronger after a cup of tea and a slice of bread and butter, she gathered her courage and resolutely went in search of her fiancé.

The library door was firmly shut and while she hesitated, her hand on the doorknob, endeavoring to screw up her courage, which was rapidly vanishing, the door was abruptly flung open and Lucius emerged precipitately, his expression thunderous. Brushing past her without a word, he ran upstairs and disappeared in the direction of his chamber.

She was still staring after his flying figure when Sir Hugo appeared in the doorway. As he saw her, his expression, which had matched that of his cousin, cleared. "Amy!" he said. "I had not expected to see you so early—"

"I have something to say—" she began quickly, before her resolution should dissolve.

"As you saw, I have just had an interview with Lucius," he said, speaking over her low voice. "The fellow's little better than a scoundrel—it only amazes me that I was fool enough not to notice it before!" He drew her into the library, and then closed the door before crossing to the window and staring out into the garden. When he turned back to her, she was dismayed to see that his eyes were a deep, glittering black, a phenomenon she had not seen for some time.

"When I told him I wished him gone from here by the end of the week, he had the gall to throw Penn's lineage in my face, producing this poster and threatening to bring my brother's widow here!" With an expression of the deepest contempt, he flicked a finger at a garish sheet of paper lying across his desk.

Amy felt a little faint as she leaned forward and read: "The Garrick Players present Miss Clorinda

Beaufort in *The School for Scandal*." The smudged, badly printed letters ran together and she had to grip the top of the heavy desk to keep from swaying. Gradually the faintness passed and she became aware that Sir Hugo was talking, unaware of her distress.

"As you are aware, my brother contracted an unfortunate alliance," he was saying, his voice bleak and his gaze once more centered blankly on the fresh morning garden. Pulling himself up and shaking his head, he began again. "It is not fair to blame her entirely. Julian was of age and not unworldly. Perhaps if he had lived, it might have worked . . . however, it was not to be. He was killed at Talavera and she arrived here with her infant, offering me the child in exchange for a sum of money, which, she informed me, would enable her to set up her own company!"

Amy made an involuntary exclamation and he raised an eyebrow. "Not a pretty story, is it? She made no secret that the alternative was for her to take the child round with her, trading on his name and the fact of his being an orphan of one of Wellington's heroes!"

Amy was shocked. "Oh, surely not! I would not believe it of . . ." Her voice trailed off as she realized it would be wiser not to mention her sister's name.

"You may well say so. I accepted guardianship of Penn, with the proviso that all should be legal and that Mrs. Beaufort and her family should relinquish all kinship with the boy. This she did willingly; indeed, she said that her family had rejected her when she took up the acting profession."

Amy could only stare at him, shocked by this further evidence of her sister's perfidy.

Seizing the poster, Sir Hugo crumpled it into a ball with a furious gesture and flung it into the empty fireplace. "I will *not* have Penn disturbed!" he said between his teeth. "The boy is happy and settled, secure in his environment. I will not allow him to be upset."

"H-how—what should upset him?" Amy asked, puzzled.

"Lucius tells me that Mrs. Beaufort has the intention of taking her son back to her maternal bosom. The perfidious wretch has suffered a change of heart!" As his words died away, he lifted his head suddenly to look full at Amy, his gaze sharp and questioning, so speculative that she found herself wondering for one dreadful moment if he already knew of her relationship to his brother's widow. Whatever she had been about to say died on her lips and she could only silently return his gaze.

"Forgive me," he said at last. "I interrupted you. You came to tell me something." He paused, watching her thoughtfully and she had the uncomfortable feeling that he knew what she had been about to say. His expression softened as he stared into her stricken face, and taking her cold hands in both of his, he continued in quite a different tone. "Believe me, Amy, I will always listen to you . . . with kindness and understanding. I want nothing, no secrets between us. . . . You need have no fear of me."

For a moment she almost confessed, hovering on the verge of telling him everything, but her courage failed as her eye fell on the bill advertising the traveling players and she recalled, with a shiver of

207

dismay, Hugo's justified anger as he recounted Clorinda's misdoings.

"I—" Her throat was dry and she had to swallow before continuing. "I came to ask . . ." She faltered under his gaze, seeking for some reason, other than the truth, for having sought him out. "To say that I have felt for some time a little uneasy about Miss James," she said, improvising quickly about a matter that had indeed been making her uneasy. "Now—now that I have some standing here, I feel I can mention something that as an employee I had no right to say."

Hugo's expression grew veiled and a hint of something that might have been disappointment appeared briefly as he turned away. "Indeed? Pray continue. You interest me."

"I believe that she drinks and that she gives gin to Penn!" she announced, unhappily, only too aware of her companion's withdrawal.

For a moment he studied her, his eyebrows drawn together in a black frown. "And what makes you suppose that?" he asked.

Now that she had started, the words came tumbling out. "His bouts of so-called illness . . . when he is so sleepy and heavy-eyed. The day he so nearly drowned in the frozen river, I had found Miss James in her room on the bed so deeply asleep that I was unable to awaken her. I—smelled something on her breath, but at the time was unable to recognize it."

"And you have now? What was it?"

"Gin," she told him briefly, without preamble.

His eyes narrowed as he stared at her without seeing her. "Leave it with me," he told her at last,

208

his voice so grim that she felt troubled for the un-suspecting woman.

"Mrs. Hill is uneasy, too," she ventured. "I would not have mentioned it—indeed, I did not feel I *could* . . . but now—"

"No need to justify yourself . . . Good God, am I such an ogre that no one dares tell me when my ward is being ill-treated? You are my future wife and as such have a position. I would expect you to bring anything that might affect Penn to my notice. I am only surprised that Mrs. Hill did not find the opportunity to drop a hint." He surveyed her rather wearily. "My only worry is what to do with Master Penn until a new arrangement can be made. . . . James Fifield has his hands full."

"I would be happy to care for him," Amy offered eagerly. "Perhaps he could eventually go to Miss Witherspoon's school?"

"Over my dead body!" was his response to this suggestion. "A tutor would be by far a better idea—but for the time being, nothing could be better than for you to take responsibility for him. If you would take him for a walk now, by the time you return, Miss James should have been dealt with."

Amy nodded her agreement and made to leave the room, but his voice stopped her as he opened the door for her.

"By the way," Sir Hugo said, taking a letter from a nearby table and holding it out to her. "This should have been left in the hall, but Hill gave it to me by mistake."

One glance told Amy that it was from her mother and her heart fluttered with guilt. As she thanked him, Sir Hugo seemed to fix her with a particularly questioning gaze, and she felt her color rise.

"F-from my mother," she faltered, feeling some explanation was necessary.

"Now, why," Sir Hugo asked lightly, bending his head, "should that bring on a fit of the flusters?" He paused only a moment, as if giving her time to reply, before going on. "Always a happy event. I'm sure you will want to read it," he said blandly, holding the door for her and allowing her to escape thankfully.

He was as good as his word, and some time later, as she and Penn returned to the house, it was to see the figure of Honora James departing in a pony and trap.

"Hooray—hooray!" shouted Penn, throwing his cap into the air at the sight of her baggage tied on behind and executing a wild dance of joy. "Horriblenora has gone!"

Amy looked more closely at him. "What did you call her?" she asked.

"Horriblenora," he answered, stopping in mid-jig to eye her warily, his gaze so innocent that Amy was convinced that he had no idea of his misnomer.

"Her name is Honora," she told him, suppressing a smile at his unconscious, but eminently suitable, nickname.

Realizing he was not about to be scolded, Penn ran ahead and was received into the welcoming arms of Mary, who hugged him fondly and whisked him up to his domain.

Conscious of the letter from her mother burning a hole in her pocket, Amy wandered away in search of a secluded place in which to read it. As she had half suspected, the missive contained a worried warning that her sister was in the area and the maternal advice to stay out of her sight. However,

her new position in the house and her awareness of
Lucius's intentions had given her new insight, and
Amy could not but feel that she, alone, could prevent the catastrophe that was threatened. The date
of the performance, which she recalled without
difficulty—indeed she suspected that it was indeli-
bly imprinted on her mind—was in two days' time.
Remembering Clorinda's usual arrangements, she
knew that the theater company would be arriving
in Winchester the previous day and at once began
contriving to meet her. Somewhat to her surprise,
Clarissa showed little interest in visiting the town,
declaring that she intended to spend the day at
home. Amy would have been extremely puzzled if
her charge had not chanced to mention that Sir Simon had expressed an intention of calling to view
the heating system of Hodge's greenhouse, which
happened to be Sir Hugo's new project, with the
idea of setting up his own and that, discovering an
unexpected interest in horticulture, she was determined to accompany them.

Miss Witherspoon was in a more flexible frame of
mind and Amy was able to persuade that lady that
the idea of paying a visit to her newly rented property was her own and that Amy had been kind
enough to agree to accompany her.

"Of course Tedbury could not refuse *you*— How
convenient it would be if you could find your
way—I should not take the liberty to ask you, my
dearest Miss Standish, if I did not know the kindness of your heart ... *pray* do not think me en-
croaching, but if Tedbury could be persuaded—"

"To own the truth, Miss Witherspoon, I have
need to go into town myself," Amy admitted, feeling

guilty, "and would be only too glad to ask for the carriage to be put to."

Consequently the two ladies set off the next afternoon, content that Clarissa would be well chaperoned by her brother and that they need have no concern save for their own business. The little country town was the usual bustling hive of people, the streets full of country folk and soldiers as well as townsfolk. Leaving Mary Witherspoon happily ensconced in the offices of Sir Hugo's lawyers, deep in the mysteries of choosing furniture and fittings for her school, and knowing that she would not emerge for at least an hour, Amy went in search of her sister.

The side door of the theater was opened in answer to her knock and upon her requesting Mrs. Beaufort, she was directed to the greenroom. Here she found Clorinda, reclining upon a chaise longue, a pair of spectacles on her nose as she perused a motley sheaf of papers.

Looking up at the interruption, she saw Amy and shrieking her name, jumped up to hug her, scattering the pages of the play in her eagerness.

"My dearest sis!" she cried, kissing her. "What a delightful surprise! How well you look." An arched eyebrow rose as she ran an experienced eye over her sibling's ensemble. "Such elegance, my dear. I vow that you match the Ton for modish fashion!"

Amy kissed her in return. "And you are as beautiful as ever," she answered truthfully. "No one would take you to be more than one and twenty."

A wary look came into the wide blue eyes and a hand was raised in warning as she glanced over her shoulder. "Ssh, my new beau is a little younger than I—and I must own to having mislaid a birth-day or two!"

She smiled roguishly, and overcome with sororal affection, Amy hugged her again.

"You bad girl!" she chided indulgently, unable to refuse her sister's winning ways. "I have news for you, too. I am engaged to Sir Hugo Dysart!"

Clorinda's eyes widened and Amy hurried on in explanation. Greatly to her relief, her sister seemed more amused and impressed than outraged.

"Amy, you sly creature!" she said, having heard the story. "I only wish you may be happy. I always found Sir Hugo both remote and arrogant, but you may rest assured that I have no intention of claim-ing Penn so you, my love, will have the felicitation of being a step-mama!"

"Why do you mention it?" asked Amy shrewdly.

"That horrid little man who visited me. Some kin to Sir Hugo, he would have me believe. Of all things, he tried to convince me that Sir Hugo wanted me to take Penn back! Of course I am de-voted to him—but I have his welfare in mind and it would not be fair to take him from a settled home. Sir Hugo wanted him and it's by far best that he should keep him. . . . Besides, I have brought Rich-ard Betteridge to the point of proposing. . . ."

Amy nodded, understanding that a small, de-manding son might well jeopardize such a proposal. She identified the "horrid little man" without diffi-culty as Lucius and put aside his odd behavior for the moment. "I think you are very wise to leave Penn where he is," she agreed, hiding her own re-lief at her sister's attitude and her disgust at Lucius's machinations.

"Dick is—would not take kindly to unexpected

213

responsibility, besides he thinks I am too young to have a son of three."

"Five!" corrected Amy gently.

"So old?" said Penn's mother, momentarily diverted. "How time flies—but, of course, I was a mere babe when I bore him."

"Oh, Clorinda, I'm your sister! Don't try to bamboozle *me*!" said Amy with a laugh. "You were eight and twenty!"

Throwing back her head, Clorinda laughed in turn. "But I always looked much younger!" she retorted.

A little later the sisters parted on very good terms. Clorinda accompanied Amy to the outer door, kissing her warmly as she stepped out into the street, before turning back herself into the theater. Smiling to herself, Amy did not notice the curricle that had been approaching and that had slowed as she appeared in the doorway; consequently she was startled to hear her name called, and upon looking round she found Sir Hugo staring at her from across the road, with a speculative gaze.

CHAPTER TWELVE

For a moment she stared at him aghast, trying to tell from his expression whether he had seen her sister or not. Raising one eyebrow quizzically, he extended a hand to her, and as the groom jumped down and ran round the vehicle to climb up and perch on the back, she took Sir Hugo's hand and made a creditable attempt of climbing into the high-sprung carriage.

"Well done," he murmured as she settled herself beside him. "What brings you to town? If I had known that you had a visit in mind, I would have willingly taken you."

Hiding her flushed countenance in the shade of her bonnet brim, Amy studied her hands. Sir Hugo had spoken lightly, but the question hung implacably in the air between them and he definitely seemed to be awaiting an answer. "Miss Witherspoon had the n-need to call on your lawyers," she improvised, intent upon a loose thread hanging from a button fastening her spencer.

"Ever the philanthropist!" he returned evenly.

"I would not have left Clarissa unchaperoned had I not thought you were taking Lieutenant Lovell round your greenhouse," she retorted. "Or so

215

Clarissa informed me, when she mentioned her sudden interest in horticulture."

"I can well imagine that you would not have come if you had known of that," remarked her companion, a shade ironically. However, he continued after the briefest pause, amusement in his voice. "As to Sir Simon . . . I thought the wind was blowing in that direction—which was why I left James to act the part of gooseberry, having no wish to sit in on my sister's romance myself. I am sure she will manage things much better without my inhibiting presence."

They drove on in silence for a while, while Amy accustomed herself to riding so high above the road. She was just relaxing a little and congratulating herself on the fact that Sir Hugo appeared not to have noticed the precise building she had left, when he returned to his original subject.

"So why, Amy, were you leaving the theater? I had not realized that you had an interest in playgoing!"

The question hovered between them, and for a moment she almost confessed the whole story to him, but her courage failed and her reply died on her lips as she recalled his earlier scathing comments about her sister.

"I—wondered if it would be possible to arrange an outing for Clarissa as a surprise," she offered miserably, hearing how feeble her excuse sounded in her own ears.

There was a long, oppressive silence, during which she stole a glance at her companion's face, finding his expression closed and his mouth tight. Slowing outside the Red Lion, he dropped off the groom, commanding him to explain to Miss

Witherspoon and Tedbury that Miss Standish was in his care, before driving on, still without a word to his passenger.

At last Amy could bear it no longer and, as they left Winchester behind, remarked brightly upon the fineness of the weather, the state of the fields, the beauty of the countryside, and the singular noise of the crows circling overhead.

"You have forgot the interesting formation of the hills to the left and that delightful barn to be seen beyond that copse of trees," he pointed out dryly. "Miss Standish, I have known you long enough to be aware that you only chatter inanely when feeling nervous."

Much struck by the truth of this, Amy stared up at him. "Oh, dear—so I do!" she said artlessly.

Gathering the reins in one hand, he covered both of hers with the other. "Let me help," he said. "Trust me, Amy."

She could have borne his anger, which she felt she deserved, but his unexpected kindness made her eyes smart with unfallen tears. A desolate sniff escaped her.

"Look at me—don't hide behind that damned brim! They can only have been invented to hide a woman's face—"

"It—it is very fashionable and cost more than I have ever spent on a bonnet," she protested, still turned from his questioning eyes.

"It is charming—and utterly ridiculous!" he replied. "It does not take a genius to see that you are unhappy—do you wish to call off our engagement?" he asked quietly. "I would not hold you to your word, if you wished to break it."

Startled, she looked up in alarm. "Oh, no!" she cried, shaking her head. "No—never!"

"Very gratifying, I'm sure. Why then the tears? Tell me what is troubling you and I give you my word to make all well. I promise you will not find me . . . unkind."

The unusual gentleness of his tone made her even more reluctant to make her confession and hear it exchanged for scorn and disgust, as she was sure it would be. Whisking away a tear, she shook her head.

"You will think me very foolish, I know—but I am tired and h-have the headache. There is nothing more."

She was aware of his withdrawal as his comforting grasp was abruptly removed and knew that in refusing to confide in him, she had lost something precious. On impulse, she turned to him and continued: "Forgive me, Hugo—I *do* have a problem, which I fear you would not understand. I—cannot share it . . . it is not wholly mine. . . ."

There was a pause and after a while he began to speak again, pointing out sights of interest and commenting evenly upon various trivial matters. Knowing she had disappointed him, Amy did her best to respond despite a heavy heart and was glad when the journey ended and she could seek the sanctuary of her room.

Clarissa appeared almost at once, throwing herself down on the bed and smiling dreamily up at the ceiling. "I really do think that Sir Simon is the most charming man," she announced. "His manners are precisely what one would wish for—so caring and gentlemanly. He makes Kit appear a callow youth. I cannot think what I saw in him. A childhood sweetheart seemed so romantic at the time—but as one grows older, of course, one's tastes change."

Amy did not reply and Clarissa sat up to look at her. Noting her pale face and strained eyes, she asked if she was not feeling quite the thing.

"I—have the headache," Amy admitted dully, finding that her excuse had arrived in truth and her skull was splitting. She wished most of all to be left alone.

"I expect it's the heat," said Clarissa knowledgeably. "I feel quite fagged myself. Shall I ask Mary to bathe your forehead with vinegar?"

Pressing her fingers to her throbbing head, Amy shook it carefully. "A cup of tea—" she murmured, realizing that Clarissa would not be contented until she had been useful, and was relieved when the other took herself off to arrange the beverage.

Falling asleep on her bed, she awoke much later to darkness and realized by the silence that she must have slept for some time and that the household was abed. Rising, she undressed and, having bathed her hot face, sat by the open window to catch the cool breeze that blew in from the quiet, moonlit garden. Whichever way she looked at her problem, she could see no way out. Consumed by guilt and misery, she wished desperately that she had found the courage to tell Sir Hugo her story . . . but the thought of seeing rejection in his eyes as he turned from her was more than she could bear, and cursing herself for a coward, she sought her bed, tossing and turning until morning, when she fell into a troubled sleep until woken by the maid's knock.

Arriving at the breakfast table, she was relieved

to see that Sir Hugo had already eaten and gone. Greatly to her surprise, Lady Myers was seated at the table, consuming large quantities of tea and sliced beef.

"Thought I'd find you here," she remarked by way of greeting. Eyeing with disapproval Amy's bread and butter, she went on: "Won't do you young gals any good, y'know. No goodness there, in that pappy stuff. If you are to provide my nevvy with an heir, you should eat good, red meat. Looking peaked, aren't you," she went on as Amy nibbled her breakfast without enthusiasm. "You and Dysart quarreled?" she asked shrewdly. "Noticed he looked like a thundercloud and near bit m'head off when I remarked on it. No respect for the older generation nowadays!"

She shook her head sadly, forking up the last of her breakfast. Throwing down her crumpled napkin, she stood up, looking down at Amy's drooping figure. "You won't want my advice—but I'll give it all the same," she said. "Don't let things fester. A good quarrel never hurt anyone. Clearing the air is a good thing, but sulking ... Have it out, my girl. Much the best in the long run, take m'word for it; besides, if Dysart's not besotted with you, I'm much mistaken ... and I fancy that you've lost your heart to him!"

Amy looked at her doubtfully and the older woman nodded sharply, pausing on her way out of the room to say: "Hugo may be a touch stiff-necked, but he's a good heart. If he liked you enough to put his ring on your finger, then tell him what's bothering you. He's astute, y'know—I've a notion that you might find that he knows already!"

Amy sat still for a few minutes after the old lady

had gone, her mind a maelstrom of conflicting thoughts, as she considered all the implications of Lady Myers's words. Suddenly unable to bear the confines of the house a moment longer, she jumped to her feet and, filled with the urge to be alone until she had made her mind up on a course of action, hurried up to her room to put on her bonnet and velvet jacket, before running to the stables.

To her relief Tedbury was nowhere in sight and a young groom obeyed her instructions to harness the gig without question, only hesitating when she declined him accompanying her, bidding him to "step aside" as she drove off.

She intended to stay within the confines of the estate and, having driven round the edge of the vegetable gardens, came out at the end of the long avenue that bounded the shrubbery. Knowing that this was one of Penn's favorite places, she was not surprised to see him among the trees, but the fact that he was in the company of two rough-looking men whom she did not recognize caused her concern. Stretching her neck the better to see, she stared intently across the intervening lawns, thinking that she must be mistaken and that the unknown individuals must be from the house or garden.

The sight of the small boy suddenly kicking out as he was scooped up by one of the men, who now seemed horridly familiar, and borne off, tucked under his captor's arm, confirmed Amy's wildest fears, and the sight of Lucius slinking off in the direction of the house did nothing to allay her anxiety. Without pause for thought, she set the pony off in pursuit across the grass, before realizing that she could not follow the men through the closely planted shrubs.

Pulling on the reins, she tried to review the situation calmly, doing her best to recall the layout of the paths and roads around the house, knowing that there was no time to go for aid.

Swinging the pony round in a wide sweep, she rejoined the road again, setting off at a good pace along the avenue to where she hoped the men would emerge. Knowing also that she was heading toward one of the estate gates, not far from the stables, she flicked the reins, urging the pony to greater effort, in an attempt to catch them before they could leave the grounds.

At first she thought she had missed them but, driving up to the gate, saw one of the ruffians in the act of leaping into a decrepit post chaise. The door was slammed shut as the ancient vehicle started off. Of Penn there was no sign, and she could only suppose that he was already in the carriage. Nearer to hand, the man had, indeed, seemed familiar and she had the dawning suspicion that he was the man who had tried to abduct the butcher's son in Winchester.

There was only one thing to be done, and without hesitation, Amy did it, swinging the pony and gig through the narrow gate and onto the road, determined to keep the speeding post chaise in sight. The little horse was game, but she knew that he could not match the two horses drawing the chaise once they reached the wider, straight main road.

Although she was sure that her quarry had no idea that they were being followed, they were obviously in a hurry and drew implacably ahead. Knowing her animal would soon tire, she was in

222

despair, when she suddenly became aware of two black heads nodding beside her elbow. A startled glance confirmed that she was being overtaken by a pair of horses, and a wild suspicion was settled as Sir Hugo drew level and then passed her.

Boxing her in against the hedge until there was nowhere for her to go, he gradually forced her to slow down. His groom jumped down and went to the pony's head as she brought the gig to a halt and, without stopping himself, Sir Hugo reached across and almost dragged her out of her carriage and into his curricle.

"They've taken Penn!" she gasped, clutching her slipping bonnet as they gathered speed again.

"Very clever, Miss Standish!" he snarled, looking ahead. "Do not try to make me believe that you are not part of this imbroglio."

"I've been trying to stop them!" Amy cried indignantly. "Why do you think I was chasing after them?"

"To join them, I presume—"

"Oh, *likely*!" she retorted scornfully. "In a gig! Wouldn't I have been in the chaise with them?"

Sir Hugo did not deign to answer and one glance at his rigid, implacable countenance told Amy that no argument of hers would persuade him other than of her implication in the affair.

By the time they reached the main road, their quarry was out of sight and could have taken either direction.

"I presume it is no good asking you which way they will have taken," Sir Hugo remarked bitingly, turning toward Winchester without waiting for her reply. After a while they came to a straight stretch of road and it was obvious from the uninterrupted view ahead that the post chaise had taken the other route.

With a muttered curse, Sir Hugo turned his horses and set off back the way they had come. With a pang of anxiety, Amy realized that they were now taking the London road, with all the chances of losing the chaise that that gave. The village of Alresford was soon left behind and then they swept through the hamlet of Chawton, barely slackening pace. Alton was reached, still with no sight of the chaise, and Sir Hugo pulled into the yard of the Crown Inn, jumping down as an ostler ran to the horses' heads.

"Why are we stopping?" demanded Amy, rising to her feet in agitation.

"Come down," he commanded impatiently and as she still hesitated, reached up to lift her down. "You have twenty minutes, no more, so make use of them, while I send round to inquire which road the chaise took. Someone is bound to have noticed."

Leaving her to her own devices, he turned to speak to the head-groom who had appeared from the depths of the stables, attracted by the sight of the prime horseflesh and expensive carriage, designed for speed.

Fifteen minutes later, Sir Hugo walked into the parlor, where Amy was drinking lemonade, a tankard of ale in his hand. "As I thought, they're on the London road," he announced coldly, his eyes glittering like jet.

As she looked up, Amy recognized the danger sign but repeated, with as much composure as she could manage, that she had nothing to do with the affair.

"A likely story," was the bitter comment. "You

conveniently arrange for Penn's governess to be dismissed, having concocted some detrimental tale about the poor woman—"

"No such thing! She was—"

"—which I believed, allowing you to take charge of Penn as you doubtless intended," he continued inexorably. "And having made the way clear, you called on your sister to finalize your plans to abduct my ward!" His eyes glinted down at her. "How very devious of you, miss—and what a besotted fool you must think me!"

"I did not—I only ever had Penn's welfare at heart."

"How convenient," remarked Sir Hugo. "An excuse for anything. Your care for my nephew excuses your deliberate falsehoods, the way you inveigled yourself into my household, undermining my influence with Clarissa, setting my family at odds ... even setting yourself up to be the future Lady Dysart!"

"Oh, no—there you are quite mistaken," declared Amy, her bosom rising with matching fury. "That you did yourself, to get the better of your aunt! *I* was merely the convenient tool." She glared at him, before tugging fruitlessly at the ring on her finger. Her hand was hot and trembling with rage and the ring refused to move. Recognizing defeat, she added defiantly that he should have it, just as soon as possible.

"Don't think to get rid of me that easily," he returned nastily, changing tack. Setting down his tankard with a snap, he advanced upon her. "You accepted my ring, and while it is still on your finger, you are my betrothed!"

"Don't be ridiculous," she cried, stamping her

225

foot and struggling anew with the recalcitrant ring. "Of all the preposterous ideas— You are the most puffed up, arrogant—*lordling* I've ever had the misfortune to meet! You cannot *want* to marry me. You just cannot bear to be thwarted! Aha!" The ring came free and with a triumphant cry, she flung it across the room.

Her aim was never at any time good and although she had intended it to fly to a far corner, the heavy ring flew up in an arc and struck the advancing man smartly upon the cheekbone just below his left eye.

With an exclamation of rage and surprise, Sir Hugo clapped his hand to his face, glared at the smear of blood that colored his fingers, and reached for Amy, snatching her into his arms and crushing her against his chest with enough force to render her breathless.

"Violence, miss?" he asked harshly. "Two can play at that game." And effortlessly subduing her struggles, he bent his head to kiss her savagely.

"The horses are ready, milord—" announced a voice loudly, as the door behind them was opened and the groom entered to stare in astonishment at the scene taking place.

Sir Hugo raised his head and his grip slackened enough to allow Amy to drag one hand free and hit him across the ear with all her strength. Seizing her hand, he forced it down to her side and shook his dazed head to clear it of the stars that lit the dim room.

"Enough," he said quietly. For a moment she thought she saw a gleam of amusement in his gaze, but all he offered was a promise to continue this later. Tossing his handkerchief to her, with the advice to wipe her face, he gripped her arm above the elbow and urged her from the room.

Finding blood on the handkerchief, Amy effected what repairs she could in her passage from the inn and hoped she was fairly presentable as they left the yard in a flurry of dust—to the obvious speculation of the interested inn servants.

"Remind me not to call there again for some time," murmured Sir Hugo dryly as they negotiated the traffic of the main street of the little market town.

Without a word, Amy proffered the square of linen and he dabbed at the cut on his cheek. "My apologies," he said briefly, looking ahead.

Hunching her shoulders, she stared out across the fields. "I had forgot that the aristocracy only felt called upon to behave in a gentlemanly fashion to their social equals," she remarked coldly, pointedly elevating her chin as she gazed over the surrounding countryside. "Of course, I now understand that being a member of the lower class, I should not expect to be treated with anything approaching civility or respect!"

"Good God, woman, you must know me better than to suppose that I think of you in any other way than as my equal!" he began, goaded—but regaining control of his temper with an effort, he continued more calmly. "Do not try me too far," he warned. "Under the circumstances, I would feel justified in setting you down in order to make better speed."

"*Justified!*" she exclaimed indignantly. "When it was *you*—when you dragged me into your curricle, with scant regard for my person or safety and—and *abducted* me!"

"Precisely," he drawled agreement, unperturbed as he tooled the carriage around the bend into the hamlet of Holyborne and then, quickening speed again, onto the open road toward Farnham.

A few miles further on, Amy felt rather than heard her companion catch his breath and, following his narrowed gaze, saw a post chaise ahead, the tired horses that drew it making hard work of the rising hill.

Watching his quarry intently, Sir Hugo nursed his own animals up the incline, urging them forward as they breasted the rise, taking care not to let them run away as the ground sloped downward. The driver ahead, who had become aware of his pursuer and who was not so careful, cracked his whip and shouted, with the result that, as it speeded downhill, the vehicle began to sway back and forth across the road, terrifying the horses into desperately attempting to get away from the fearsome thing behind them.

"Stop it—drop back!" cried Amy, clutching at his arm. "They'll overturn!"

As she spoke, the inevitable happened and she watched in horror as the chaise hit the grass verge, bounced, lifting a wheel high into the air, and fell onto its side, the momentum of the frightened horses dragging it for several yards.

The driver, who, by an incredible feat of luck or athleticism, had leaped from his perch onto the back of one of the animals as the carriage fell, held on for dear life and was swiftly carried out of sight as the aged traces snapped under the strain.

Pulling his snorting pair to a halt a short distance from the accident, Sir Hugo flung the reins to Amy with a brief order to hold them, leaped to the ground, and ran to the fallen chaise. As he approached, the door that now faced heavenward was flung back against the side and a man's head and shoulders appeared in the opening. Seeing Sir Hugo, he scrambled out and stood briefly upright, before launching himself onto his pursuer, carrying him to the ground with the weight of his body.

With her heart beating a violent tattoo, Amy stood up the better to watch as the two men rolled in the dust, each striving for supremacy. Suddenly she became aware that another figure had emerged from the chaise. As he crouched on his haunches, reaching back into the interior, she recognized him as the man from Winchester. A wriggling, squirming smaller figure was hauled out, and rising to his feet, the man tucked a wildly kicking Penn under his arm and scrambled to the ground.

Avoiding the fighting men, he charged in Amy's direction, becoming aware of her standing in the curricle. For a moment he hesitated, before apparently deciding that she presented no danger; he showed blackened teeth in a wolfish grin and came on.

Looking round for a weapon, Amy saw at her feet the long whip Sir Hugo had discarded in his haste, and raised it above her head. Eyeing her sideways, the man scuttled by, and praying that her old skill had not deserted her, she struck suddenly with the whip, the leather thong catching the man's ankle and wrapping itself round it like a snake. Pulling on it with all her strength, Amy jerked him off his feet, shouting for Penn to join her, as his captor lost his balance and fell heavily.

With a wild shriek of excitement, Penn ran across the road and clambered up the wheel like a monkey to hurl himself into his aunt's arms. Giving him a brief but heartfelt hug, Amy pushed him behind her and prepared to face the man, who had scrambled to his feet and was creeping menacingly toward them, an ugly expression on his face.

"Keep away," warned Amy, raising her weapon threateningly and, as he still came on, flicked the thong toward him, leaving a bloody cut on his cheek.

The man caught the thong as it wrapped round his wrist and, with a sudden jerk, dragged the whip from her grasp. The evil smile appeared again as, with a snarl of triumph, he hurled himself toward her.

Amy had a brief glimpse of his hands, with fingers crooked like talons, stretched up to her, and instinctively shrank back, still clutching the reins in one hand. The horses, sensing her distress and already disturbed by the fight that had taken place around their hooves, jibbed and started forward, causing her to give all her attention to halting their intended flight.

When she could return her attention to other matters, it was to become aware of Penn shouting shrill encouragement as his uncle, having disposed of the first ruffian, turned the full force of his fury on the other.

At first Amy thought Sir Hugo would triumph easily, but already tired from his previous encounter, he was obviously finding this second flight no easy matter. Realizing that she would have to take action, she climbed down from her high perch, tied the reins to a branch of a convenient tree, and, first scooping up a suitable stone, made her way warily to where the struggle was taking place in the middle of the road.

For a moment she studied the dust-covered participants as they rolled around, first one and then the other uppermost. Choosing the moment carefully, she waited until the abductor straddled Sir Hugo, apparently intent upon strangling him, and lifting the stone above her head with both hands, brought it down with all her strength on the black, greasy hair.

A satisfactory dull thud ensued, but at first she thought her blow had had no effect, for the man remained upright. Then his grip on Sir Hugo's throat slackened and he fell slowly backward, his expression suddenly blank.

Struggling for breath, Sir Hugo sat up, eyeing first his supine enemy and then Amy, who still clutched her weapon.

"The—fellow over there shows signs of recovery—would you care to finish him off, too?" he asked dryly as he climbed to his feet.

"Are you all right?" she asked, going to his aid. "Good Heavens, what a fright I've had!"

"Not half so much as I, when I saw you looming over us with that fearsome boulder raised on high," he retorted, gingerly feeling his bruised throat. "I'm only thankful that you hit the right head!"

"Oh, I was very careful," she assured him, carelessly tossing the stone aside, missing by an inch the first man who had blearily raised his head.

Encouraged by this, he scuttled across the road on his stomach, climbed to his feet when he judged himself at a safe distance, and began to make his escape at a shambling run.

"What fun!" cried Penn, hurling himself onto his

unsuspecting uncle. "Shall I bite that man again?" he asked hopefully, as Sir Hugo recovered his balance.

"Again?" he inquired, shuddering. "Most certainly not—I'd say once was quite enough."

"Y-es," agreed his nephew. "He didn't care for it. He called me an—an awesome whelp."

"Yes, well, I think you had best forget about that," Sir Hugo said hastily, having a good idea as to what the man had said.

"He's very nasty," continued Penn with a dispassionate air. "I learned lots of new words—"

"I expect that as you've been so brave, Sir Hugo might allow you to help him hold the reins," put in Amy quickly, successfully diverting them both from all thought of the newly acquired vocabulary.

"Brat!" said Sir Hugo fondly, tossing him up into the curricle. Turning to Amy, their eyes locked for a second as he took her hand to assist her, then, "Wretch," he murmured for her ears alone.

Coloring at this endearment, she put her foot on a spoke of a wheel and accepted his help as she climbed into the vehicle.

"But—where are we going?" she cried as they started forward, not back as she had expected.

"To Farnham," Sir Hugo replied calmly.

"Oh, no! We cannot," Amy exclaimed, suddenly conscious of the picture she must present, with her bonnet dangling from its strings down her back and her hair fallen about her shoulders. Sir Hugo, she saw, was in an even worse state; one eye rapidly closing, his cut cheek already swollen, his once-pristine neckcloth showing clear signs of the recent ill treatment it had suffered. "You've lost your hat," she told him inconsequently.

Brushing his disordered curls away from his damp forehead with a grimy hand, Sir Hugo thrust the two ends of his crumpled neckcloth impatiently inside his coat. "The horses are blown," he said. "We'll stay the night in Farnham."

Amy stared at him, aghast. "But—what will people think?" she gasped.

"Precisely what I tell them," he replied with a return to his former arrogance and she fell silent, cuddling Penn against her for their mutual comfort.

She found that, despite his dishevelment, Sir Hugo still had an unconscious air of quality about him, that with the obvious value of his equipage caused the landlord of the inn to accept his consequence without question, and she and Penn were quickly escorted to a bedchamber where she could repair the ravages of the recent adventure, while Sir Hugo informed the local magistrate about the villains inhabiting the area.

After a bath and a supper of chicken and jelly, Penn fell quickly asleep, and leaving him in the care of the landlord's competent daughter, Amy went in search of her own meal. Knowing that she could easily have requested it to be brought to her room, she felt that there was still much to be settled between herself and the baronet.

He was standing by the fireplace as she entered the parlor, reminding her of their first meeting.

"Well, Amy?" he greeted her, coming forward to lead her to a chair.

Raising her eyes to his face in a searching glance, she studied him silently. What she saw there made her sigh a little and, catching her breath, look down at her hands clasped in her lap.

233

"I must confess to having been very ... foolish," she murmured.

"Yes," he agreed. "You should have trusted me."

"But—Mama and I were led to believe you an unfeeling monster, determined to separate us from Penn. Deception seemed the only hope. And then it was too late to tell you. I could not bear the thought of your rightful disapproval of my actions."

"Foolish girl, indeed. I knew all along. Did you really think that I was not aware of your sister's real name?"

She looked up at that, a question in her green eyes. "But—why did you let it go on?"

"I must confess to an interest as to what you intended and felt it better to have you where I could see and deal with anything that might arise. To be honest, you were unlike any governess I'd previously known and I allowed myself to be intrigued by the way you managed my wayward sister ... and soon I found my own interest aroused. While somewhat surprised by the rage Aunt Augusta's assumption caused me, I was not averse to finding myself engaged to you. Indeed, I knew that I rather cared for the idea!"

Amy blinked, her heart beginning to quicken. "Why did you believe me capable of aiding in Penn's kidnapping?" she wondered aloud.

Sir Hugo had the grace to look shamefaced. "You must admit it all rather tied in—it appeared that it was possible that I was mistaken in you ... and my wretched temper did the rest. Good God, woman, you didn't make things easy!"

"It was all Lucius, you know. I saw him in the grounds with the men who took Penn. He slunk off as I drove after them."

"I know—that was when I confronted him with my suspicions!" exclaimed the baronet, clenching his fists. "The fellow was such a coward that it took only minutes to get the truth from him, once he saw that I was in earnest." Sir Hugo looked so grim that Amy was surprised to feel a fleeting sympathy for Lucius. "The wretch was after Clarissa as a bride—and Penn's estate, which would come to her in the event of the child's death. When that scheme fell through with the arrival of Sir Simon and Clary's total rejection of Lucius at the dance, he decided to fall back on an old idea, engendered by the attempted kidnapping of the child in Winchester, and arranged to have Penn abducted in order to save his West Indian estates with an enormous ransom, which I would pay for Penn's safe return. Much good his machinations did him," he said with satisfaction. "Cousin Lucius is now in the care of Tedbury and James on his way to Bristol, where he will be put on board a ship bound for the Caribbean! I've had suspicions ever since our visit to Malreward Castle. There was something deuced odd about the way he was creeping up on the boy . . . and that turned my mind to that business on the river. I even began to wonder if you were in collusion with him!"

"With Lucius!" exclaimed Amy, unable to hide her revulsion.

"I admit it was not the most likely of partnerships and I soon discarded the idea," he continued blandly, "to decide that you were your mother's spy, with no more evil intent than to report to her upon her grandchild's health and well-being." Shooting her a glance, he hesitated momentarily before going on with less than his usual self-confidence.

235

"With this in mind, I visited Portsmouth and took the liberty of calling upon her. . . . I may say we got on famously and that I returned with her full approval of my making a proposal of marriage to you."

Astonished, she stared wide-eyed at him and was glad to see the first flicker of doubt that she had ever seen in his gaze—perhaps Sir Hugo was not totally impervious to others' feelings after all. Before she could speak, however, he stepped forward to take her hands in a grip that hurt.

"Darling girl," he began, his voice harsh with emotion. "Miss Standish—Amy, you cannot be unaware that I love you! You have no idea how glad I was when that damned ring stuck! You would make me the happiest of men if you will take it back and marry me. Clary tells me that you are the only hope of making me an agreeable person—indeed, she says she has never liked me half so well as of late. For her sake, if not mine, you should accept my offer."

Amy smiled at the half-teasing note in his voice, recognizing with a pang of joy the affection it concealed. Reading her answer in her face, Sir Hugo swept her into a crushing embrace, kissing her soundly, to the satisfaction of both, until something she had said earlier suddenly returned to rankle in his mind.

Lifting his head, he stared down at her. "Lordling?" he said, on a note of interrogation. "*Lordling!* You called me a lord*ling*!"

Amy smiled lovingly up at him. "Yes," she agreed. "Does it matter?"

The baronet considered. "Not in the least," he said, and kissed her again.

236